"You're not alone," Neal said. **"You have friends to help you. Including** ~~me.~~**"**

"You~~~~

"Of ~~~~

Unea~~~~ firmation. He s~~~~ ~~the promises~~ he couldn't keep. But he could help her with Ian without getting involved. Their kiss notwithstanding. It could be fun watching the little guy grow, knowing he wasn't his responsibility.

The sun moved out from behind the clouds, its bright rays emphasizing the tears drying on Anne's cheeks. He resisted an urge to wipe the last of them away with his thumb.

Her lips quivered. "You're right. I have to think of Ian, honor my friend's wishes."

Neal would have liked to see her a little more fired up. Her friend had entrusted Anne with her most important treasure. At least, he thought of his daughter that way. Raising her hadn't been easy. But there wasn't a time since her birth that he hadn't wanted her with his whole heart.

He looked at Anne, so small and slight in the shadows of the towering willows.

Yes, he would help her.

Books by Jean C. Gordon

Love Inspired

Small-Town Sweethearts
Small-Town Dad

JEAN C. GORDON's

writing is a natural extension of her love of reading. From that day in first grade when she realized *t-h-e* was the word *the,* she's been reading everything she can put her hands on. A professional financial planner and editor for a financial publisher, Jean is as at home writing retirement and investment-planning advice as she is writing romance novels, but finds novels a lot more fun.

She and her college-sweetheart husband tried the city life in Los Angeles, but quickly returned home to their native upstate New York. They share a 170-year-old farmhouse just south of Albany, New York, with their daughter and son-in-law, two grandchildren and a menagerie of pets. Their son lives nearby. While Jean creates stories, her family grows organic fruits and vegetables and tends the livestock du jour.

Although her day job, writing and family don't leave her a lot of spare time, Jean likes to give back when she can. She and her husband team-taught a seventh-and-eighth-grade Sunday-school class for several years. Now she shares her love of books with others by volunteering at her church's Book Nook.

You can keep in touch with her at www.Facebook.com/JeanCGordon.Author, www.JeanCGordon.com or write her at P.O. Box 113, Selkirk, NY 12158.

Small-Town Dad

Jean C. Gordon

Love Inspired

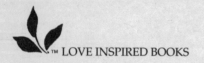 ™ LOVE INSPIRED BOOKS

Recycling programs for this product may not exist in your area.

ISBN-13: 978-0-373-81670-5

SMALL-TOWN DAD

Copyright © 2013 by Jean Chelikowsky Gordon

All rights reserved. Except for use in any review, the reproduction or utilization of this work in whole or in part in any form by any electronic, mechanical or other means, now known or hereafter invented, including xerography, photocopying and recording, or in any information storage or retrieval system, is forbidden without the written permission of the editorial office, Love Inspired Books, 233 Broadway, New York, NY 10279 U.S.A.

This is a work of fiction. Names, characters, places and incidents are either the product of the author's imagination or are used fictitiously, and any resemblance to actual persons, living or dead, business establishments, events or locales is entirely coincidental.

This edition published by arrangement with Love Inspired Books.

® and TM are trademarks of Love Inspired Books, used under license. Trademarks indicated with ® are registered in the United States Patent and Trademark Office, the Canadian Trade Marks Office and in other countries.

www.LoveInspiredBooks.com

Printed in U.S.A.

Call to Me and I will answer you, and I will tell you
great and mighty things, which you do not know.
—*Jeremiah* 33:3

I will instruct you and teach you in the way you
should go; I will counsel you and watch over you.
—*Psalms* 32:8

To all of my "children": Carrie Jean, Caelin, David-John, Druhan and Nathanael, with thanks to my agent, Diana Flegal, my editor, Melissa Endlich, and my critique group BFS for helping me realize my dream of writing inspirational romance.

Chapter One

His guard unit's tour of duty in Afghanistan had prepared Neal Hazard to face just about anything. Except, evidently, returning to the classroom after seventeen years. He looked down the hall of the main building of the Ticonderoga campus of North Country Community College and wiped his hands on his jeans. How had he ever let his daughter, Autumn, talk him into starting college?

"Hey, Dad," Autumn called from behind him.

Just what he didn't need, more of her help.

She hurried over, followed by a young man and woman. "This is Sean and Lindsay."

He nodded to the couple. He wanted to know Autumn's friends, but he wanted to get this advising meeting over with.

"So, did you meet with your advisor?"

"No, I'm on my way to her office now." He took a step toward the room.

"Have you gotten your books yet?"

Autumn's voice took on the oh-so-patient tone he'd often used with her when she was small. "You know NCCC has a virtual bookstore. You could order them online and have the books shipped to the house. I could stop by later and help you."

"I don't even have my schedule finalized yet. But I'm sure I can handle it." *I handled the transport of supplies for hundreds of troops. I can order a few books online.*

Autumn wrinkled her nose.

"Bummer," Sean said. "That happened to me my first semester. The schedule thing. The biology book had to be back ordered, so I didn't have it for the first few days of classes." He squeezed the hand of the girl next to him. "Fortunately, Lindsay let me share her book until mine came." The boy gave Neal a knowing look.

Neal coughed to hide the chuckle that erupted deep in his belly. He didn't think he'd be making the kind of social connections Sean was intimating.

"And, Dad," Autumn said. "Keep next Friday night free."

Neal racked his brain for what they had going on next Friday and came up blank.

"Us upperclassmen are hosting a get-together for the freshmen at the Saranac Lake student center." She grinned at him with the smile she'd used a thousand times before to wheedle something out of him.

She must be razzing him. She couldn't think he'd go to a party for a bunch of eighteen-year-old kids.

"Or, if you can't make it, maybe your truck could? Jack's scheduled to be on call with the tow truck that night, so I don't have any transportation."

Jack was Autumn's longtime boyfriend and nearly constant companion. Her socializing without him wasn't a bad idea, even if it involved Neal's truck. "Sure, I can't see any reason why not. I don't have any plans."

"Thanks, Dad." She hugged him.

He pulled away with an uncomfortable feeling that people were staring at them.

"You *could* come with me. You know, since you're not doing anything anyway." Again with the smile.

Why didn't he have a normal kid who was embarrassed by her parents and avoided them in public? "I'll think about it."

Neal Hazard. Anne Howard read the pop-up on her computer alerting her to her next student appointment. Her thoughts went back to her sophomore year of high school. She and her mother had spent that year with her grandmother in Paradox Lake in the Adirondack Mountains of New York, not far from North Country Community College. Her parents had separated—again.

A Neal Hazard had been her practice partner for the Schroon Lake High School Science Olympiad team. She did the math. Her student appointment *could* be Neal's son. If so, he was taking after his dad. Anne remembered that Neal had wanted to be an environmental engineer.

A knock on her open office door drew her attention.

"Dr. Howard?" An attractive man about her age strode across her office and offered his hand.

Anne rose to accept it.

"I'm Neal Hazard."

Her hand went limp in his, and his smile stiffened.

Of course. The sandy brown hair, short and neat in an almost military style. Hazel eyes that had held hers in a virtual vise. He was taller, broader than the last time she'd seen him. But he'd been seventeen then. He must be thirty-six now.

She tightened her grip and finished the handshake. "Anne O'Connor Howard." She waited to see if the use of her maiden name would elicit a reaction.

He blinked. "Annie? Annie O'Connor?" His smile widened.

Her heart quickened. He did remember her.

"I never would have recognized you."

"It's been a long time." She motioned him to the seat in front of her desk. "We can catch up while we wait for your son."

She wouldn't have pegged the Neal Hazard she'd known in high school to become a helicopter parent, but who was she to judge—as long as he didn't interfere with her curriculum. If he'd followed his college plans, he'd have as many years of environmental engineering experience as she did. But the new environmental studies program was her baby.

"My son?" Confusion spread across his face. "You mean Autumn, my daughter? She's not meeting me here." His expression cleared. "She's a second-year nursing student, not environmental studies."

"Then, why…the appointment?"

He shifted in the chair and tapped his finger on the metal binder he'd placed on her desk in front of him. "For my student advisement."

This Neal was her *student* Neal Hazard. "What happened?" she blurted, and immediately wanted to crawl under the desk. Michael had schooled her—successfully she'd thought—on curbing her impulsiveness. To be professional at all times.

"I mean, you talked about going to Rensselaer Polytechnic Institute." That wasn't any better. Obviously, her training had completely deserted her. But the Neal she'd known had such big plans.

He set his jaw. "Autumn happened. Not that I regret that for a minute."

"I'm so sorry. I didn't mean to be rude." She modulated her voice into her most professional tone. "You're here to have your class schedule approved?"

His masculine features hardened into a neutral expression. "Yes. I took a couple of math and science courses online. The credits transferred, but I need your signature to substitute them for the program requirements to take the 200-level conservation course."

He flipped open the binder and pulled out several papers that he pushed across the desk to her. "My transcripts and proposed schedule."

She scanned the schedule. The only class on it that she was teaching this semester was the conservation one he needed her permission to take. Her gaze moved to the transcripts. Maybe the courses wouldn't match the prerequisites. Then she wouldn't have to have him in her class. Teaching someone she'd dated, even if it was years ago and only a couple of times, wasn't something she was prepared for. Her North Country environmental program was a clean slate, something she wanted to do all on her own, with no baggage from her past.

Her stomach dropped. The classes were interchangeable with the North Country requirements. "The classes look fine. Let me check online registration to see if the conservation class is filled. It was close to full yesterday."

He nodded.

Anne clicked into online registration. The class was closed to additional students, with a waiting list that wasn't long enough to add another session.

"Sorry, it's full," she said a tad too brightly.

Neal raised an eyebrow.

"I can put you on the waiting list. We might be able to work out an independent study if there's not enough to add another session." Preferably taught by someone else.

"Do that." He held her gaze, adding a belated "Please."

She focused back on the computer screen and typed in the necessary information.

"Here you are." She signed his schedule and handed the papers to him. "You can register at Admissions while you're here on campus or do it online."

He stood. "Thanks." Neal paused, his lips parting slightly like he was going to say something else.

"It was good seeing you again," she shot out to fill the momentary silence.

"Yeah, see you around."

Anne slumped in her chair as he turned to leave. She'd been so sure that heading up the environmental studies program had been God's plan for her to get past Michael's sudden death, his infidelity and the shaky business practices it had exposed. A chance to succeed on her own. Neal Hazard was a complication neither her hard thinking nor her prayers could have taken into account. But, as she'd come to understand, she'd read God's desires wrong before.

Neal walked into the kitchen of his parents' house. His home. The familiarity soothed him. But it was time—past time—for him to get a real place of his own. Before Autumn had gotten an apartment in Ticonderoga with her best friend, Jule, living here had made sense. Now, even though he had his own apartment over the garage, it struck him as just plain juvenile.

"Hi." His mother breezed in. "How was school? Did you get all the classes you wanted?"

"All but one." He winced at how similar the conversation was to their usual interchange when he'd come home from high school. Deciding to make up for lost time, to do some of the things he'd missed by becoming a father so young, hadn't meant he wanted to regress to adolescence.

He stopped himself from rummaging in the refrigerator for an after-school snack. "You'll never guess who I ran into."

"Someone from high school? I told you you wouldn't be the only older student."

"Annie O'Connor."

"That sweet girl you took to the prom?"

Neal tried to remember Anne as she'd looked then. They'd been more friends and teammates than boyfriend and girlfriend. What had attracted him to her was her quick mind. All he could picture was her beautiful waist-length strawberry-blond hair and the ugly glasses that she'd had a habit of repeatedly pushing up on her nose when she was nervous. A far cry from the poised woman he'd met with this afternoon. Her shoulder-length hair had darkened to a rich light brown. And without the glasses, her expressive dark-fringed eyes transformed her looks from average to beautiful.

"Yep, only she's *Dr.* Howard now, my student advisor."

Mary Hazard made a choking sound and covered her mouth with her hand before bursting out in laughter. "Oh, Neal, seriously? Was it terribly uncomfortable for you?"

Neal scratched the back of his neck. At thirty-six years old, he wasn't up to after-school sharing time with his mom. "Not any more than it was for her. She thought I was my son."

His mother's forehead creased in confusion.

"Now that's an interesting proposition." His very pregnant sister, Emily, waddled into the room. "Like that riddle. Brothers and sisters have I none, but that man's father is my father's son…"

"Hey, Jinx." He purposely called her by her childhood nickname to irk her.

She lowered herself into a chair at the table. "Go ahead."

"When Annie—Anne—saw my name, she thought the Neal Hazard she had an appointment with might be my son."

"Oh, no," Mom said.

"So, old man," Emily teased, never missing a chance to point out the eight-year difference in their ages. "Was she surprised when you walked in?"

"No. She thought I was there to meet my son and sit in on her meeting with him. Can you imagine what Autumn would do to me if I tried that?"

Emily faked a shudder. "I don't even want to think about it."

"Me either," their mother added. "I've got to run. I'm taking Edna Donnelly to her doctor's appointment in Ticonderoga. You'll have to bring Annie by sometime now that you've reconnected." With a quick wave, she left.

"Looks like Mom has that all mapped out for you, probably right down to a playmate for this guy." Emily rubbed her belly.

"Hardly. She's Dr. Howard, not Dr. O'Conner. Her husband might have something to say about that."

"Or maybe not. The interview with her that I read

in the *Press Republican* didn't mention her husband. She could be divorced or widowed, I suppose."

"Still not a chance."

"Not a chance of you going out or not a chance of you helping me fulfill Mom's dreams of a houseful of grandchildren?"

"I've done my part already with Autumn. No more kids for me."

"So you say now. But, with the right woman… Want me to do some digging? Find out for sure if Anne is single?"

"No. Dr. Howard is the head of the environmental studies program and my advisor to boot. Even if she is single, I'm sure the college has rules against instructors and students fraternizing."

"Fraternizing?" Emily laughed. "I think that's officers and enlisted personnel. Remember, you mustered out of the National Guard after your tour in Afghanistan."

He wasn't likely to forget that.

"But you are interested. I can see it in your eyes."

What was it with women that they were always interpreting everything into feelings? His mind flashed back to Anne. At least, to the Annie he *used* to know. She thought more like a guy.

"You're not the typical North Country student. I'm sure it wouldn't be any problem if you are interested."

He glared at his baby sister.

"What? Assuming she's single, you're her peer."

Age-wise, yes. Career-wise, not by a long shot. And it bothered him. But the fact he was bothered bothered him more. He'd been perfectly happy with his electrician business until Autumn had put the idea of going back to college in his head.

"No, I don't think Dr. Howard and I will be traveling in the same social circles."

"Come on, big brother. You can't tell me you're not a little interested."

Emily was right. He couldn't tell her that.

Anne dabbed on a little mascara and lip gloss and inspected her face in the mirror. What had possessed her to let her next-door neighbor Jamie talk her into going to the Singles Plus group Bible study at Jamie's church? Since relocating to the Adirondacks, Anne had been looking for a church to attend, but she wasn't ready for any kind of singles' scene. Michael's betrayal and death were still too fresh for her, even though it had been over a year.

She ran a comb through her hair and tucked it in her bag. Jamie had insisted the group was all about fellowship, not people looking for spouses. In fact, Jamie wasn't even single. Her husband was in the army and had recently deployed back to the Middle East.

Anne heard a knock at her back door, followed by Jamie's friendly, "Hello."

"Be right there," Anne called back. She stopped and checked her reflection in the full-length mirror one more time before heading downstairs to join Jamie. She pushed the bridge of her nose, an old habit left over from when she'd worn glasses. Michael had insisted she wear contacts. Her tailored slacks and short military-style jacket were all wrong. Maybe a quick change into her blue linen dress.

"Anne?" Jamie called.

"Coming." The suit would have to do.

Her fears of being overdressed were confirmed when she saw Jamie in her jeans and a hooded sweatshirt over a bright pink T-shirt.

"Sorry to rush you," Jamie said. "It's just that Bible study is my one chance to escape from children for a couple of hours. Between the kids at school and their various ailments and my three, I don't get much adult me-time."

"I understand," Anne said with a twinge of guilt because she didn't. Not really. Jamie's three kids were adorable and so well behaved. And she made handling them by herself, plus her job as the school nurse, seem a breeze. Wanting to escape her kids struck Anne as more in line with her own parents' disinterested parenting style than Jamie's loving one.

She followed her neighbor out to her slightly battered SUV. With Jamie's husband away and no relatives nearby, Anne could see how Jamie would want some adult time, someone to share her day with. For all that Michael's death and the aftermath had put her through, she still missed having someone to come home to after work.

Jamie moved a couple of marbles, a Dora the Explorer pencil and a pink sequined purse off the passenger seat so Anne could sit.

"Opal's," Jamie explained.

Anne didn't think she'd ever seen Jamie's four-year-old without her pink purse. "Can she survive the evening without it, or do you want to stop and I'll run it into the house to her?"

"She has her favorite babysitter, Autumn, tonight, so I think she'll be able to soldier through."

The drive to Hazardtown Community Church took about ten minutes.

"I think you're going to fit right in," Jamie said as they walked across the parking lot to the church lounge. "A lot of us are transplants, but a couple of members are natives. Maybe you'll know them from when you went to school here."

"That was a while ago, and I kind of kept to myself, since I didn't know how long we were going to be here. We moved around a lot." No need to give her all the gory details about why.

About ten people were in the lounge sitting around a coffee table when they entered.

"Hey, I brought a visitor. Everyone be on your

best behavior. We don't want to scare her away. This is Anne Howard, my new next-door neighbor. She works at the community college."

"Hi," Anne said.

Jamie went around the circle, starting with a blonde woman who looked about Anne's age. "This is Erin Ryder. She's the high school guidance counselor."

She moved on to an attractive dark-haired man sitting on the couch next to a very pregnant woman. "Emily and Drew Stacey. They're another exception to the single rule. They joined before they married, and it seemed dumb to make them leave afterward. Emily is a graphic artist, and Drew runs the new Sonrise Camp and Convention Center at Paradox Lake."

Emily gave Anne a thorough once-over that ended with a quirky smile.

Jamie finished the introductions and offered Anne a seat on the couch next to the couple before taking a seat in a folding chair across from her. "Looks like we're all here except our leader."

"Does the pastor teach the class?" Anne liked the idea of meeting the pastor informally before hearing him preach.

"Not quite," Emily said, prompting chuckles from the other members of the group.

Anne resettled herself on the couch and clutched

her Bible in her lap. Apparently, this was some kind of private joke.

"We take turns," Emily said. A smile played with the corners of her mouth. "Our leader for the study we're starting tonight is my brother, Neal."

Neal burst into the room, kicking himself for being late for his first night as leader. "Sorry. Mrs. Donnelly blew a fuse at her house and couldn't get ahold of her son to come and replace it for her. I stayed an extra few minutes to explain to her that the fuse box should be replaced with circuit breakers."

"Mrs. Donnelly was our high school English teacher," Emily said to the woman sitting next to her. "And maybe our Dad's, too." She laughed.

His sister's explanation drew Neal's attention to the woman. *Anne.* He placed his lesson manual and Bible on the table with a thud.

"Anne, I didn't expect to see you here."

"So, you know each other?" Jamie asked.

"Yes. We went to high school together," Neal said.

Anne nodded. "We hadn't seen each other in years, until this afternoon. Neal is in my environmental studies program at North Country."

Neal glanced around the room, expecting everyone to be looking at him. No one was.

"Let's get started," he said. "Pass this around

to Anne." He handed a study guide to the person next to him rather than directly to Anne across the table from him. It was probably petty, but the less personal contact with her, the better for his state of mind. His attraction to her wasn't anything more than a lingering remnant of happy times before he met Autumn's mother and he'd had to grow up fast.

"We're studying Job," he said for Anne's benefit. "And we open with prayer." Neal started to sweat. Anne—Dr. Howard—was making him nervous. He'd better make the prayer particularly heartfelt.

Neal bowed his head. "Dear Lord, help us to learn from Job's trials and tribulations, to hold steadfast to You, and not question what we see as obstacles in our life path but recognize them as part of Your plan to help us grow in our faith and love. Amen."

Neal glanced at Anne as he lifted his head. She still had her eyes closed and hands folded in her lap. Had his prayer hit home with her? She opened her eyes and he looked away.

"Who wants to read?" he asked.

"I will," Emily said.

While his sister read, he stole another glance at Anne.

"Should I keep reading?"

"Huh?"

Neal met his sister's gaze. She smirked.

"No. Thanks." He'd get her later, as only a big

brother could. "We'll pick up on the next book after we consider the questions on page nineteen."

Neal continued the study, ruthlessly redirecting the focus whenever comments got off point and uncharacteristically dominating the discussion. At a little after eight-thirty, he wrapped it up with a closing prayer.

With her husband's help, Emily pushed herself to a standing position and turned to Anne. "You and Jamie are staying for refreshments, aren't you?"

"I don't know." Anne gave Jamie a questioning look.

While he hated to lose a potential new member, it might be better if Anne didn't join the group permanently. They all got along so comfortably.

"We sure are," Jamie said. "I have Autumn until ten."

"Great. There's coffee and hot water for tea in the church hall kitchen," Emily said. "And Erin brought her double-chocolate brownies. I'm starved."

"You're always starved," her husband, Drew, teased.

"And whose fault is that?"

Everyone laughed.

"You go ahead," Drew said. "I'll be there in a minute." He hung back with Neal while the others headed to the kitchen to get drinks.

"Nice work," Drew said.

Neal glared at him.

"What? I mean it. She hung on your every word."

"I was *not* trying to impress Anne."

"Of course you weren't. You just had a lot to contribute tonight. More than you have in the past six months combined."

"I really prepared for the lesson." Neal ground out the words. He and Drew had been friends even before he and Emily had fallen in love. But the guy was getting on his nerves big-time tonight.

"Don't fight it. You'll be way ahead of the game. I know."

"I'm not fighting *it,* because I have nothing to fight."

"Sure. Whatever you say." He smirked just like Emily had earlier.

Neal grabbed his books. This conversation wasn't worth wasting his breath on. He turned to leave, but the returning group congregating by the doorway blocked his escape. He'd hoped to slip out with some excuse to Drew while the others were getting coffee.

"I'm going to go get some coffee," he announced to no one in particular and wove his way out of the room, staying clear of his sister and Anne.

The kitchen was empty and blessedly quiet. Neal poured the last of the coffee in a cup and heaped in two teaspoons of sugar. He took a swig. The sugar didn't help. The beverage tasted like what it was. Cheap swill that had sat too long on a burner.

He took another sip and grimaced. Drew hadn't been completely off base. Neal did have an interest in Anne that he couldn't seem to shake. But it wasn't what Drew thought. And it wasn't anything he was going to pursue. They were simply old friends. Anne had gone to Schroon Lake Central only one year.

Laughter drifted out of the lounge as he approached. Then he heard Anne's voice.

"So, if you don't think I'm too nosy, when are you due?"

"Feels like it should have been a month ago," Emily answered, "but I still have another couple of weeks to go."

"If you're on time," Jamie chimed in. "I was almost two weeks late with Opal."

Neal's heart warmed. Not his Autumn. She was a week and a half early. He remembered like it was yesterday. Being called out of Mrs. Donnelly's English class to report to the office. His father waiting there, tapping his fingers on the counter, not wanting to tell Mrs. Wood, the office manager and local busybody, what the family emergency was. Mom and Vanessa had gone ahead to the hospital. Neal had been scared out of his mind, but seeing his daughter enter the world had been indescribably awesome.

"No, don't even say that." Emily's voice resounded

up the hall and brought him back to the present. "I couldn't take it."

Neal heard the low rumble of his brother-in-law's voice, but the women's laughter drowned out his words.

"How about you, Anne?" Emily asked. "Do you have kids?"

Neal halted at the doorway and fixed his sights on Anne. He hadn't thought about her having kids. Only about her husband. Neal had decided he was some high-powered exec. Made his latent adolescent crush on her even more ridiculous.

Her mouth curved with a sadness echoed in her eyes. "No. I've always wanted children. But my late husband and I didn't have any."

She was a widow? He ignored the elation that rushed through him and grabbed on to her next words as protection against his attraction to her. Of course she wanted children. Almost all women wanted children. One more shield in his arsenal against pursuing something that couldn't be.

Chapter Two

"Neal was sure in a rush to leave this evening," Jamie said as she and Anne were driving home.

Because of me, no doubt. Anne rubbed the bridge of her nose. She wasn't sure what she'd done besides mentioning her meeting Neal at the college earlier in the day. After that, he acted really odd given the old Neal she'd known. But people changed. She certainly had.

"He usually stays for the social hour?"

"Yeah. And he was acting strange during class, too. Talkative. He usually throws out an idea or comment and lets everyone else dissect it. I think he was nervous."

"About leading the study?" That didn't seem like the Neal Anne had known.

"No, about an old flame…"

"We aren't old flames."

"You did go out in high school, though."

"We were on the Science Olympiad team and went to the junior prom."

Jamie slapped the steering wheel. "I knew it. I've never seen a woman have that effect on Neal before. Not that every eligible woman in Essex County hasn't tried."

Anne didn't need Jamie pointing out how attractive Neal was. "That was a long time ago." A lifetime ago.

"So you *are* interested."

"He's one of my students. It wouldn't be ethical."

"Come on. He's not an eighteen-year-old kid."

"No, I'm certain there's a clause in my contract." Even if there wasn't, Anne could use her position to keep her distance. If that's what God wanted her to do. This time, before she entered any kind of relationship, she'd ask for His guidance. When she'd met Michael, she'd been too new in her faith, and he'd been so overpowering.

She was just getting back on track with her beliefs and her life. A life not dominated by Michael, but still shaded by his lies and deceptions. Lies not only to her but also to the people who worked with and for him. People who still worked for her. She needed to keep her actions perfect because that was the right way to live, and she didn't want any of Michael's filth to taint her program. Her work here might help undo some of the damage Michael had done.

Jamie shifted the SUV into a lower gear and turned the corner to their road. "Oh, I'm sure there are perfectly acceptable ways to get around that if you want."

But she didn't want to get around things. And she didn't want to be part of a couple again. At least, not yet. She needed time to be herself again.

"Neal said he has a daughter," Anne said, hoping to change the direction of the conversation.

"Yes, Autumn. She's my babysitter tonight."

"He's divorced?" Anne tried to keep her tone casual. Michael had been divorced, too. Not that it mattered. While she thought that a lot of people didn't work hard enough at their marriages, some people, like her parents, simply weren't meant to be married in the first place.

"No." Jamie drew the word out.

He couldn't be married. Jamie wouldn't be pushing him at her if he were.

"Stop looking at me like that," Jamie said. "He's not married. What kind of person do you think I am?"

Her friend laughed, but Anne cringed inside.

"Autumn's mother took off when Autumn was a couple of months old. The week she and Neal were supposed to be married. No one heard from her for years, not even her parents."

"That's terrible. Was she from around here?" Anne tried to picture the girls she'd met the year she went to Schroon Lake Central. She couldn't help thinking that he hadn't wasted any time taking up with someone new, after her mother had taken her back to Boston that June.

"No, Emily said she was from somewhere near Chicago. She and some friends had rented a cabin for the summer. Obviously, she came from money. You know what the camps on the lake cost for a week." Jamie stopped until Anne acknowledged that she did with a quick nod.

"Vanessa—that's her name—was a year or so older than Neal. A college student on summer break. She went back home at the end of the summer. I don't know all of the details. Only what Emily's told me. But Vanessa came back that winter after she'd found out she was pregnant. She and her parents had fought and she showed up in town unannounced. The Hazards let her stay with them."

"I remember Neal's parents."

"Good people."

"So Neal's parents raised Autumn?"

Jamie pulled into the driveway of Anne's rental house. "Neal raised Autumn. I guess you don't know the Hazards well."

Jamie's words slapped her. It was a reasonable assumption, wasn't it? Neal must have been about seventeen. She knew too many men a lot older who wouldn't have stepped up like that. Her husband, Michael, hadn't been very involved with his children from his first marriage. Work had been more important.

"I mean, his mom watched her while Neal was at school and, then, when he was at work. He did some kind of electrical apprenticeship with his uncle's friend. Neal wouldn't have had it any other way. He gave up a scholarship to some college near Albany."

RPI. Rensselaer Polytechnic Institute. Neal's dream college.

"They were so young," Anne mused. Everyone had thought she was marrying too young at twenty-two, before she'd even finished her master's degree. "They were barely out of high school. No wonder they didn't make it."

"Actually, Neal was still in high school when Autumn was born. But, I don't think their age was the biggest problem. John and I started dating when we were sixteen and married the summer after we graduated high school. Twelve years later, we're still together."

Anne bit her tongue. She'd let her mouth get the best of her and insulted Jamie. Maybe Michael had been right. She needed a keeper.

"No," Jamie picked up where she'd left off. "Emily said Vanessa was unstable. *Scary-crazy* were her actual words. But she's remembering through the eyes of a ten-year-old."

"Poor Neal."

"Good thing he's not around to hear that."

"But he missed out on so much. He gave up his scholarship to RPI."

Confusion spread across Jamie's face.

"Rensselaer Polytechnic Institute. That's all he used to talk about. How he wanted to go there."

Jamie shrugged. "You do what you have to do. He's going to college now, just a few years later than planned."

Almost twenty years later and at NCCC, not world-renown RPI.

"Besides, if you ask him, he'll tell you he has no regrets. He wouldn't trade having and raising Autumn for anything. If you had kids, you'd know what I mean."

Her friend's unintentional barb stung. She'd wanted kids. Still did, if the right man came along. A vision of Neal, his face lit with recognition when he'd realized who she was this afternoon, filled her mind. Anne blinked the image away.

Jamie stopped the car by Anne's side door. "Want to come over and meet her? Autumn?"

Anne hesitated. "Some other time. I'm beat."

"Sure. And my invitation is still open to come to church with us on Sunday. You've met some of the other members now, and I know you'll like Pastor Joel. Everyone does."

"Hazardtown Community Church is on my list."

She'd made a list of local churches to visit until she found one that felt right. "I'll let you know."

Anne let herself out of the car and waved goodbye to Jamie. She couldn't get Neal's situation out of her mind. NCCC wasn't RPI, but she'd developed a good environmental studies program and could make sure Neal had every opportunity to make the most of it.

A cool gust of wind swirled the leaves on the driveway around her feet. She unlocked the door and flicked the light switch. The kitchen overhead fixture came on, then faded and flickered before returning to full power. She'd told her landlord about the problem, and he'd said he'd have someone come to check it out. She'd call him again in the morning.

The light flickered again and went out. Maybe she should call Neal instead.

Standing in the dark, she pictured herself and Neal sitting in this room at the kitchen table when her grandmother owned the house, quizzing each other for an Olympiad meet.

A shiver ran up her spine. The thought of Neal in her home, working for her, was almost as unsettling as having him as her student.

She'd call her landlord.

Anne frowned at the black pickup truck parked in the driveway in front of her garage the following afternoon. She'd left a message for her landlord this morning, but he hadn't called her back to say he was sending someone over. Of course, he might have called her house phone. An octogenarian and former friend of her grandparents, Harry Stowe didn't seem to grasp that he had a better chance of reaching her on her cell phone or at her office phone number.

She pulled beside the truck and shut off her car. A bright yellow lightbulb logo on the truck door proclaimed Let Lake Electrics Light Your World. She hesitated getting out. Maybe she should go over to Jamie's. The school bus had driven by Anne going the other direction. So Jamie would be home from work. Harry should have cleared things with her before he let the workman in.

A familiar bespectacled face topped by wispy white hair peered out from behind her living-room drapes. Harry. Anne placed her hand over her heart as if that would stop the pounding. She grabbed her briefcase, stepped out of the car and started toward the house. Enough time had gone by that she should be more used to living alone.

Harry had the door swung open before she got to the steps. "Come on in. I put water on for tea."

"Thanks." She wasn't entirely comfortable with the older man making himself so at home, even though he owned the house.

He pulled a chair out at the kitchen table for her and went back to the stove.

The kettle whistled. A cup of tea would be nice. She dropped her case on the counter by the door and sat at the table.

Harry placed a mug in front of her and a matching one on the opposite side of the table. "I didn't see any cookies," he said, his voice rising in question.

"No, sorry." She sipped her tea. "It doesn't seem worth the effort to bake only for me."

"It's probably for the best." He lowered himself into the other chair. "I'm not supposed to have them anyway."

Her companion stared into his mug of tea, his eyes slowly closing. Had he fallen asleep?

"Your grandmother made the best chocolate chip cookies."

Anne started, a wave of tea slopping over the top of her mug. She jumped up and grabbed a paper towel to mop it up.

"She used to bring them into school and leave them in the faculty lounge." He smacked his lips together in remembrance.

"You taught with Grandma?"

"I was the high school principal." His eyes went soft. "Why, I remember the day she…"

Anne geared up for one of Harry's stories about the good old days.

Then, there was a clang of something hitting the

cement floor, followed by a muffled male voice, reverberated from the basement.

Harry paused. "The electrician is replacing the fuse box with breakers. A young fella."

From Anne's experience with her landlord, young could be anyone from a teenager up to her parents' age.

"Edna Donnelly recommended him. She taught with your grandmother. Seemed to think he needs the work. But who doesn't in today's economy?"

Anne swallowed her mouthful of tea. The man working in her basement had to be Neal.

"She's hired him to work on her wiring, too. I was skeptical when he said he could come right over today. It sounded like he has no other customers. But Edna's known him his whole life and says he's the best. That's good enough for me."

Footsteps sounded on the basement stairs.

Anne gripped her mug.

"Done already?" Harry asked as Neal entered the kitchen.

He stopped abruptly when he saw Anne. "Not quite. I need some different gauge wire to run from the well pump to the breaker. It's out in the truck." He looked at the door as if considering how quickly he could be out of it.

"This is my tenant, Anne Howard. Her grandmother used to own this house."

"I know," Neal said. "I didn't recognize the address right off. But as soon as I passed Jamie's place and saw the house, I remembered."

Anne fixed her gaze on the tea mug. What had he remembered? The last time he'd been here? He'd been treated to one of her mother's phone tirades with her father. She raised her gaze to find him staring at her, his hazel eyes soft. He *was* remembering her mother's scene and pitying her, like he had that night.

She straightened in her chair. Not everyone had parents like the Hazards. And she'd done just fine with her life, at least with her professional life. She had a successful career. Two of them, in fact.

"So you know each other," Harry said.

"We went to high school together," Neal said.

"The one year Mom and I lived here with Grandma," Anne corrected.

"I don't remember that," Harry said. "Must have been after I'd retired." He took his glasses off and squinted at Neal and Anne.

Neal's mouth twitched as if he were struggling not to smile.

"I knew all of my students by name when I was principal." Harry replaced his glasses. "Nope," he pronounced.

"Mr. Arnold was our principal," Neal said.

"Arnold. Yeah. He did okay. I had my reservations when he was hired. He started out as a gym teacher, you know."

Anne didn't know if it was his age or his personality, but Harry didn't hesitate to share his thoughts. *Politically correct* was not a phrase in his vocabulary.

He shielded his mouth and leaned across the table, dropping his voice to a loud whisper. "I didn't know if you'd be comfortable with a strange workman in the house. That's why I stayed. But, since you two are old friends, I can see you'll be fine."

The half smile left Neal's face.

Harry straightened. "I'm going to head off," he said at full volume. "Edna invited me for dinner."

Anne bit back the words that sprang to her lips. Harry might be a townie snob, but wouldn't be that thoughtless on purpose. And she was sure Neal wouldn't appreciate her defending him.

"You can leave your bill with Anne, and I'll stop back for it tomorrow. Nice meeting you, Neal."

"Nice meeting you."

The older man left.

"He didn't mean it," Anne said.

Neal's eyes narrowed.

"The workman thing."

He pressed his lips into a thin line.

"And about Mr. Arnold only being a gym teacher."

"I know. So, Harry's an intellectual snob. I'm going to get that wire for the pump connection."

He crossed the distance to the door in three

long strides. She bit her lip. Was she an intellectual snob, too, pointing out what Neal obviously already knew?

Neal slammed the top to the toolbox shut. So that's what Anne thought of him? He wrapped the wire around his hand. Harry's remarks hadn't bothered him that much. He was from a different generation. But when she made excuses for the older man, it was too much. He gripped the wire. He'd made his choices, choices he believed God had guided him to make. And most of the time he had no regrets.

Then, there were the few other times, like now. Anne's dark-fringed eyes shimmered with unspoken emotion. Pity. It had to have been pity. Those times got him longing for things he'd given up and couldn't recapture. Winning his fourth letter in baseball. He'd been too busy to play his senior year. Hanging out with the guys. The degree from RPI he'd once coveted.

He trudged up the stairs, wishing he had entrance to the house though the cellar doors out back instead. When he got to the kitchen, Anne was gone. His tense muscles relaxed. Anne, or maybe it was the whole college thing, dredged up feelings Neal thought he'd shed years ago. One thing he knew for sure, as soon as he had his schedule ironed out with her, he was going to switch academic advisors. A switch he was sure Anne would readily agree to.

Okay, she was a coward. Anne had stayed upstairs until she heard Neal's truck pull away. When she went downstairs, his bill was on the table. She flicked on the kitchen and outside lights. Both came on immediately at full power with no flickering. She'd expected no less. He'd also left his business card. She didn't know why that surprised her. He was a business owner. But Harry already had Neal's number. Had he left it for her? A small tremor shook her hand as she picked it up.

The lightbulb graphic and *Lake Electrics* script matched the sign on his truck. Anne smiled. Below his business information was a quote.

And God said, "Let there be light," and there was light. God saw that the light was good, and He separated the light from the darkness.
—*Genesis* 1:3–4

Anne rubbed the card between her thumb and forefinger. At Michael's insistence, she'd scrupulously kept her faith and business separate. Wouldn't want to offend a client. She admired Neal for being so upfront *and* for pursuing the college experience he'd had to forego as a young adult.

She tucked the card in her pocket. As his academic advisor, she was going to do everything she could to make his college career a success.

Chapter Three

Neal pulled on his favorite long-sleeved T-shirt and well-worn jeans in anticipation of the college mixer. Not his first choice for a Friday night. But, for whatever reason, Autumn wanted him there. Maybe she just wanted company on the long drive to the main campus center in Saranac Lake. It wasn't as if he had a heavy social schedule. In fact, all he'd done the past few weeks was go to classes, work, study, work. If nothing else, it would be fun seeing Autumn having a good time with her friends.

Autumn waved from her upstairs window as Neal pulled into her driveway. When he was deployed to Afghanistan last year, she and her best friend, Jule, had rented the in-law apartment above Jule's aunt's garage.

"Hey, Dad," she said as she hopped in the truck. "Thanks for coming early. I want to make sure everything is set up like it's supposed to be. I wish I could have found someone to swap clinicals with me this afternoon, so I could have gone over and supervised. Jack would have taken me before he went into work."

"I'm sure everything is fine."

"It probably is, but I'd feel better if I'd been there to supervise. I am the committee chair." She glanced at her watch. "We should get there early enough for me to make any adjustments."

"You know who you sound like now, don't you?"

Autumn laughed. "Don't tell me. Gram?"

"Okay, I won't tell you." He got a kick out of seeing his mother and sister in his daughter. Looking at her, Neal had trouble absorbing that this poised young woman was his baby girl.

"So, how are your classes going?" she asked.

"Not bad. Jeff Lawler and I are still working out the independent study in conservation."

Neal had been relieved when he'd gotten his final schedule for the semester and saw that Jeff, and not Anne, was the supervising instructor for his independent study.

"He thinks he may be able to get me a work study with Green Spaces. That's the engineering firm that's assessing the environmental impact of the new birthing center Adirondack Medical Center is building in Ticonderoga."

"Sounds cool. You're a hands-on kind of guy anyway."

Neal tightened his grip on the steering wheel

and pressed down on the accelerator to pull around a car that was going just under the speed limit. Hands-on as opposed to intellectual? He'd gotten the same vibe from Anne's landlord, and from her a little, too, for that matter. It made him want to point out that he'd been the salutatorian of his high school graduating class. He'd had early admission to RPI. Neal loosened his grip on the wheel. But that was all in the past. And truth be told, he liked being an electrician, having his own business.

"Yeah, it should be cool." So far, the independent study promised to be the most interesting class this semester. The other classes were easy. He might as well be taking them online. But he'd wanted the whole college experience. And he was going to get it if it killed him, starting with this mixer thing tonight.

"Will Dr. Howard be meeting you at the mixer?"

Neal glanced at Autumn out of the corner of his eye to see if she was busting on him. She did take after Jinx. The teen's expression was neutral.

"No, why would you ask?"

"She RSVP'd, so I just thought…"

"Why?"

"You're seeing her, aren't you? Jack saw your truck at Dr. Howard's house and says you drive by his house about every day. He figured you were going to Dr. Howard's up the road."

"My truck was at Dr. Howard's because her landlord hired me to replace the fuse box in the house. And I've been over that way dropping Myles off for Jamie on the days I've had jobs in Schroon Lake. He's running cross-country. It saves Jamie and the girls from having to go back and pick him up after practice." No need to mention the couple of times he'd stopped over at Anne's afterward to check on how her lights were working. He could imagine how Autumn would view that. Anne hadn't been home either time.

"Oh," Autumn said in a small voice. "I was kind of hoping you were dating."

Now Autumn *really* sounded like his mother. "Anyway, Dr. Howard should be there, and some other instructors."

"So I won't be the only old person."

"Let's just say there'll be some age-appropriate people there."

"Watch it. I could change my mind and turn around."

"Daddy! You wouldn't."

"You know I wouldn't."

"Yeah."

"Brat!"

For the rest of the drive, he half listened to Autumn fuss about the arrangements for the mixer and contemplated the other "age-appropriate" people who might be there. He certainly hadn't planned to spend the evening with Anne. They'd been doing a good job of avoiding each other since he'd done the work at her house. She hadn't come to Singles Plus for the past two weeks or to Community Church last Sunday. Jamie had said Anne was shopping around for the right church. Not that he'd asked— exactly.

Neal checked out the dashboard clock as he turned onto the campus. "Since it's so early, I'm going to drop you at the student center and run over to the electrical supply store and pick up a few things."

"All right. I should have enough help without you." Her eyes narrowed. "You're not going to bail on me, are you?"

"No, I'm not bailing. I should be back in a half hour."

He stopped in the nearly empty campus center parking lot and watched Autumn until she was inside. No matter how old she might be, she was still his little girl.

The half hour turned out to be more like an hour. When he returned, the sun had gone down and the parking lot was at least half-full. Inside, the hum of voices vied with the DJ's music selections to produce an almost deafening din.

"Hey." A couple of guys from one of his classes waved him over. "You didn't say you were coming."

"My—" He stopped himself before he said "my daughter talked me into it." "Last-minute decision."

"Us, too. Nothing else much going on," Tyler said.

"Check it out!" Ryan interrupted.

Neal automatically followed the guy's gaze and spotted Anne. She was a little old for them, but he couldn't argue with the sentiment. Anne *was* looking good. Her gauzy blouse in muted fall colors and tailored chocolate-brown slacks should have made her look out of place in the sea of T-shirts and jeans. But on her, the dressier clothes looked perfectly Anne. Even in high school, she hadn't been a fashion slave like so many of the girls.

"That blonde talking with Dr. Howard is hot."

Neal hadn't noticed anyone with Anne.

"Maybe we should head over that way," Ryan said.

"Not me. I get enough of Howard in class. There are plenty of other hot chicks here."

Neal would have found Tyler amusing if he weren't dissing Anne.

"What's wrong with Dr. Howard?" Neal asked during a lull in the music, booming over the other voices.

A few heads turned in his direction. Maybe he could leave now and pick Autumn up later. He'd put in his appearance for her. His gaze shot back to Anne. She was still talking with the student. He released a pent-up breath.

"Obviously, you aren't in any of her classes,"

Tyler said. "She's so tight. Doesn't cut anyone any slack."

"You've got that right." Ryan launched into a litany of wrongs Anne had committed. To Neal, her actions sounded like an instructor keeping her class under control and making sure she covered all the course material.

"Come on, guys. I know for a fact Anne can be a fun person."

Both guys gave him a strange look.

"We went to high school together."

"Get out!"

Before Neal could jump to her defense, the band struck up an old slow song. The haunting strains took him back nearly two decades to the Schroon Lake High School gymnasium and Annie in his arms at the junior prom.

"Prove it," Ryan said. "I'll ask the blonde to dance. You ask Dr. Howard."

"Ha!" Tyler scoffed. "I dare you. I say you both get shot down."

"You're on." Neal's words were a lot more confident than he was.

"I think this is our song." Ryan sidled up to the blonde who favored him with a dazzling smile.

Anne frowned at the interruption. The young woman had approached her and asked about four-year colleges with good environmental engineering programs. So few women were interested in engineering. She'd thought she'd found a protégée. From the way the woman was so easily distracted by Ryan, perhaps she'd been wrong. Anne had always put her career first, even as a student.

A familiar deep voice broke into her thoughts. "Actually, I think it's *our* song."

"Neal."

Ryan's eyes popped, and Neal smirked. Something was going on here that she wasn't sure she wanted to be part of.

"Would you like to dance?" Neal's mouth curved into a real smile.

She shouldn't, especially after the way she'd been silently chastising the woman she'd been talking with for dropping their conversation to accept Ryan's invitation. Besides, Neal was a student and far too attractive in a metal-gray T-shirt with a dark stripe that accented his broad chest. His faded jeans hugged his slim hips. She fiddled with a button on her blouse, suddenly feeling overdressed.

Without waiting for a verbal assent, Neal took her hand and led her toward the other couples who were dancing in front of the DJ's stand. She glanced furtively from side to side to see if anyone was watching them before allowing the song to take her back to a simpler time. A time when being asked, or not asked, to dance could make or break a girl's world.

Neal's arms slid around her waist and she rested her hands on his shoulders and stepped close to him. It had been a long time since a man had held her in an embrace, and she missed the feeling of protection. But this man was Neal Hazard, not her husband, Michael. She stiffened and put more space between them. Neal looked down at her quizzically, and her face flushed. She turned her head away to the side and let the music wash over her. It was only a dance. Neal was an old friend. Nothing more.

Anne shivered at the song's end when Neal released her and stepped back, breaking the cocoon of warmth that had enclosed her.

"Would you like a drink?" he asked. "I could use a soda."

"Me, too." Her parched throat and dry mouth made the words come out in a squeak.

As they walked over to the refreshment table, a petite girl with long blond hair gave them what looked like a thumbs-up as they passed by her. A goofy grin spread across Neal's face, then settled into a half frown.

"My daughter, Autumn," he explained. "I'll introduce you after we get our drinks."

"Sure."

It was hard to believe Neal had a college-age child. Many of her college friends and colleagues had kids now, but they were all babies or in elementary school. And in their eleven years of marriage, she and Michael had barely gotten to the think-about-a-baby stage.

"Cola or ginger ale?" He held up a can in each hand. "Or it looks like they have some kind of punch, too."

"Yes, cranberry." A girl behind the punch bowl held up a ladle full.

"I'll take that."

The girl handed her a cup, and Anne took a sip. The tangy liquid was cool and refreshing. Who would have thought a slow dance would leave her so thirsty?

Neal opened his soda with a *pop.* "Everything good with your lights now?"

"No problems at all."

"Good." He shifted his weight from one foot to the other. "I stopped by the other evening to check, but you weren't home."

Her stomach tingled. The punch hadn't seemed that carbonated.

"Everything is light and bright." She gulped the rest of her punch, not believing she'd actually said that.

"Hi, Dr. Howard. Hey, Dad, having a good time?"

Neal's daughter was beautiful. Her white-blond hair and petite stature must be from her mother, but Anne could see Neal's sister, Emily, in Autumn's eyes and heart-shaped face. And Autumn's mischievous grin was pure Neal.

"How could I not be?" He glanced from Autumn to Anne.

Warmth bubbled through Anne.

"Anne, this is my daughter, Autumn."

"Nice to meet you."

"You, too," Autumn replied.

Neal gestured around the room. "You know, Autumn set this all up." His pride came through in his voice and radiated from his face.

"Not quite all of it. I let a select few other people help me."

Anne joined in Neal's chuckle. Autumn sure was Neal's daughter. At least the good-humored, take-charge Neal she'd known in high school.

"And, before I forget, you can leave early if you want." Autumn tilted her head toward Anne. "I can catch a ride back to Ticonderoga with one of the kids in my anatomy class, so you don't have to stay to the bitter end."

"Neal," someone called from behind him. Tyler came bounding across the room waving his hand.

Neal turned to run interference while Anne and Autumn chatted on. He gave Tyler a tight shake of his head.

"I thought you'd left without my congratulating you."

Obviously, he'd been too subtle. Neal glanced sideways at Anne and Autumn. Anne met his gaze.

"I didn't think either you or Ryan had a prayer of a chance."

Anne kept her gaze focused on him. Prayer might be a good idea.

"Who would have thought—"

The band chose that moment to take a break, reducing the noise in the room by several decibels.

"—that Dr. Howard could loosen up like that. Way to ace a dare, man." Tyler pounded him on the back.

"I enjoyed meeting you, Autumn." Anne's voice rang over the hum as clear and cold as a high peaks January morning. "Tell your *father* I had to go home and grade papers."

"I messed something up, didn't I?" Tyler asked, his expression contrite.

Neal watched Anne leave through the main door. "Yeah, but not as much as I did."

Chapter Four

"Hello! Anybody home?" Emily's voice echoed up the stairs and down the hall to Neal's apartment.

He pried open his eyes and scowled at the alarm clock. Eleven-fifteen. He stretched and shook off the last vestiges of the sleep he'd finally achieved about dawn. The last time he'd slept in this late was probably before Autumn was born. He wanted to recapture the life he'd lost, didn't he? But minus the teen angst.

"Mom? Dad?" Emily sounded more urgent.

Neal pulled on some clothes and descended the stairs two at a time down into his parents' living room. Emily's due date was next week, and her husband, Drew, had been called to New York City on business. Although it seemed to Neal that babies usually came late, Autumn had been early.

"Are you okay?" he asked as he hit the floor next to her. With her waist-length hair down, rather than pinned up as she usually wore it, his little sister looked about Autumn's age—too young to be having a baby.

"I'm fine." Her voice hitched and she lifted her hand to her belly.

"You're sure?"

"I've been having false labor all week. It'll stop in a bit. Where's Mom? I want to borrow a couple of eggs to make brownies for Drew. He should be home this afternoon."

"I don't know. I just woke up."

"Late night?" she teased.

"Not really. I went to that college mixer thing Autumn wanted me to go to." And tossed and turned all night once he'd gotten home. He debated whether to tell her about the debacle with Anne. Get a woman's view on it.

"Oh, yeah, Autumn told me you were going. She seemed to think you were meeting Anne Howard there." Her eyes lit in question.

How many people had Autumn said that to? It was probably all around town by now. He shoved his hands in the front pockets of his jeans. He was in enough hot water with Anne already without making her the subject of local gossip.

"Well?" Emily rubbed her belly.

"No, I wasn't meeting Anne. I went as a favor to Autumn. She wanted me there for whatever reason." He still hadn't figured out why.

"So was she there?"

"Who?" Neal asked, fully knowing who Emily meant.

She rolled her eyes. "Anne."

"Yes."

"And?"

He cleared his throat. He might as well tell her or she'd pester him all day with questions. Or, worse, hear about it from Autumn—or Anne herself. Neal crossed his arms and replayed the evening to Emily, from his conversation with Tyler and Ryan to the dance with Anne and her abrupt departure.

"Big brother, you are an idiot."

"What?" As if he didn't know. He just didn't want to admit it.

"Come on. Don't you remember my senior prom? Matt Norton took me on a dare from his football buddies. I found out after we got there."

"I didn't dance with Anne because Tyler dared me. I wanted to."

Emily glared at him, reminiscent of Anne before she left the mixer. "The next day when you found out from Mom, you were ready to teach Matt a lesson or two."

He swallowed, remembering how outraged he'd been on his sister's behalf. "It is sort of like that."

"Sort of?"

"Okay, just like that. Except I didn't plan it."

"The hurt's the same."

"We're only friends." His statement probably sounded as lame to Emily as it did to him.

"It's okay to hurt friends?" Emily didn't wait for his answer. "All the more reason to apologize to her."

Shame washed over him. He'd been thinking more along the lines of avoiding Anne to make it easier on both of them. "You're right. I will."

Emily doubled over and hugged her belly. Neal looked over at the clock on the DVR. "Hey! That's like your third contraction in ten minutes. How long has this been going on?"

She waved him off. "I told you, I've been having Braxton-Hicks contractions, false labor, all week."

He glared down at her. "How long?"

"Since early this morning."

"You need to get to the hospital."

She breathed in deeply and blew the breath out. "The contractions will pass. They always do. I'll make the brownies to get my mind off them. Drew can take me to the hospital when he gets home if I'm still having contractions then."

Neal wiped his palms on his jeans. The hospital was a good hour away.

"We're going now. Call your midwife. What's her name? Kelly?"

Emily nodded.

"We'll stop by your place for your hospital bag."

Tears welled in her eyes. "But I need Drew. Or Mom. Where's Mom?"

"I don't know." He gritted his teeth. "They don't check in and out with me."

"But I need a labor coach," Emily said, a hint of hysteria working its way into her voice.

Neal swallowed hard. "I could do it. It hasn't been all that long since Autumn was born, and I know the process hasn't changed."

"Eww. You're my brother."

Like he was any happier about this than she was? "When will Drew be back?"

She sniffled. "In a couple of hours. He planned to leave the city about ten."

Vanessa had been in labor with Autumn for hours. Drew would be back for the important part. "It'll be fine."

She bit her lip and her eyes widened.

Another contraction so soon? "You can call Kelly on the way to your house." He hustled her out to his truck.

As Neal had figured, Emily's midwife told her to go to the hospital. And on the way, Drew called from a gas station near Warrensburg to say he'd left earlier than expected and would be home in about forty minutes. Emily told him to meet them at the hospital. Her smile when she put her phone back in her bag broadcast her relief loud and clear. The rest of the drive sped by, helped along by Neal's heavier than usual foot on the gas pedal.

When he turned off the truck in the hospital parking lot, Emily shoved a handful of papers and her medical insurance card at him. "Here, take this stuff. You can take care of admitting me. We already filled out all of the preadmission forms."

He took the papers and guided her to Labor and Delivery.

"Hi, I'm Emily Stacey," she told the motherly looking nurse at the desk."

"We're expecting you," the nurse said. "You're our first baby in two days. I'm Liz. Let's get you into a room. Then, we'll call your status in to Kelly. She's on her way."

Liz turned to Neal. "Mr. Stacey, please wait here. Jenn, the other nurse on duty, should be right back. She'll go over all of the admission information with you and bring you in."

"I'm Emily's brother, Neal, not her husband." He could have added that he wasn't at all sure he wanted to be brought in.

"Drew should be here in a half hour or so," Emily explained. "And you—" she pointed at Neal's chest "—can man up and keep me company until he gets here."

Right. Now that they were at the hospital, and his offer to be a substitute coach was looking less and less inviting to him, Emily wanted to take him up on it.

"It's not like I'm going to drop this baby in the next half hour." Emily looked to Liz for confirmation.

"That's what we need to get you into your room and checked out for." Liz guided Emily to a room a couple of doors down from the nurses' station.

Neal walked down the hall to the water fountain and took a long drink. Then he paced back to the station and studied the painting on the opposite wall. Looked like Ausable Chasm. Probably a local artist. He started to cross the hall for a closer look.

"Mr. Stacey?" A young woman in scrubs who looked barely older than Autumn, walked up the hall to him. "I'm Jenn."

It struck him that she might not be much older than his daughter. Next summer Autumn would be a registered nurse.

"I'm Neal Hazard, Emily's brother. My brother-in-law should be here soon. I have the information for her admission." He waved the handful of papers his sister had given him.

"We can sit over here." She indicated a desk next to the wall behind the station counter.

Neal answered all the questions and provided the required insurance card.

"That should do it. I'll go see if they're ready for you yet."

"Okay. I need to call our parents and let them know Emily's here."

"You can use the waiting room if you want some privacy. I'll be here at the desk when you get back."

"Thanks."

Neal took his time walking to the waiting room, alternately worrying about Emily being alone and hoping Drew got here by the time he'd finished calling Mom and Dad. The nurse, Liz, would stay with Emily, wouldn't she? She'd said they hadn't had any babies in two days. Wouldn't that mean they had no other patients?

He sat in one of the pastel-colored vinyl upholstered chairs and leaned his elbow on the wooden armrest with his cell phone to his ear. It rang through to his parents' house.

"Hi, Mom."

"Neal. What's up?"

"I'm at the medical center with Emily."

"The baby." She squealed. "Everything okay?"

"Yeah, the nurse is getting her settled in a room. Kelly isn't here yet."

"Have you talked with Drew?"

"Em did. He was about forty minutes behind us, near Warrensburg."

"How long have you been there?"

Neal checked his watch. "About twenty minutes."

"We must have gotten back to the house just after you left. We were at the grocery store."

If he'd only known. They could have waited and Mom could have come as Emily's backup coach. He looked at his watch again. Drew wouldn't be here for another twenty minutes.

"Hon?" his mother said into the silence. "Shouldn't you go be with your sister until Drew gets there?"

Did he have a choice? "Yeah, I'd better."

"Your dad and I will be there in about an hour. Give Emily a hug and tell her we're praying for her and the baby."

"Sure thing." He almost asked her to pray for him, too, if Drew didn't get here in time.

Neal returned to the nurses' station. "You'll need to wait a minute to go in," Jenn said. "Her water broke. Liz is getting her into a clean gown. She's further along in her labor than we thought."

"Yeah, she was trying to ignore the contractions until her husband got back from a business trip to New York."

The nurse laughed. "Looks like she did a pretty good job of it."

Neal swallowed hard. "She's not going to have the baby right away, is she? Has her midwife gotten here yet?"

"Probably not, and no, Kelly is still on her way."

"So is my brother-in-law." *I hope. He has to be.* "I shouldn't be so spooked. It's not like I haven't done this before."

"Oh, how old is your baby?"

"Nineteen. She's a nursing student at North Country Community College."

Jenn went on without batting an eyelash. "That's where I went. I graduated last spring."

Neal felt old. He'd expected at least a little surprise that he had a daughter that old.

"What's her name? I probably know her."

"Autumn Hazard."

"Tiny blonde?"

"That's her."

"Neal." The other nurse came up beside him. "Emily's asking for you."

"She's okay, right?"

"She's fine. Her contractions are steady. She's eight centimeters dialated. It'll probably be a couple hours."

"Good. Her husband should be here anytime now."

The corners of Liz's mouth twitched as she obviously suppressed a smile. He needed to stop saying that.

Neal walked the few steps to Emily's room and pushed the door open. She was standing at the window. "Looking for Drew?"

"Yes."

"He'll be here soon. Want to watch some television?"

"Saturday afternoon TV? I don't think so. Let's take a walk."

"Sure." Whatever she wanted to do to kill the time until Drew got here.

"We could go look at the babies, but from what Liz said, I don't think there are any."

He followed Emily into the hall.

"Drew," she shouted to a figure coming up the hall and took off at a fast waddle.

"Her husband," Neal said to the grinning nurses.

"We guessed," the older one said. "That gets you off the hook."

"You've got that right. If they're looking for me, I'm going to the cafeteria to get some coffee."

Jenn pointed down the hall in the opposite direction of Drew and Emily. "Go past the nursery. The stairs to the right will take you directly down. Or you can take the elevator to the lobby and follow the signs."

"Thanks." He took off in the direction of the stairs. A woman stood in the empty hall in front of the nursery window looking in. He slowed his pace. The delicate profile, her perfect posture. She looked a lot like Anne. But what would Anne be doing in Labor and Delivery? He needed coffee more than he'd thought.

She turned and her eyes widened in surprise. "Neal."

He shot off a prayer. *Lord, forgive me for my behavior at the mixer and give me the wisdom to come up with the right words to apologize to Anne for any hurt I've caused her.*

If only she could be half as forgiving as he knew his Holy Father was.

"Hi. You're still talking to me," he blurted. *Not the best start.* "I'm so sorry about last night. I really did want to dance with you."

"Let's forget it." Her expression remained neutral, but her eyes clouded.

Regret pierced his heart. He deserved it. Her dismissal was for the best. It wasn't like he was looking for his apology to do any more than put them back on an acceptable business/social footing. At least that was all the rational, adult side of him was looking for.

"What are you doing here?" he asked, attempting to close the growing chasm of silence between them.

She didn't seem to notice that his words came out as a demand rather than the conversational question he meant. Her features softened. "Harry asked me if I wanted to ride along with him to visit Edna Donnelly. Not that he isn't perfectly capable of driving up here himself. His words."

"Of course. Is Mrs. Donnelly all right?"

"She had pacemaker surgery this morning. Harry said she expects to be released tomorrow. But they have a standing Saturday night date, and he felt he had to keep it."

"Good man."

"They're cute together. I wanted to give them some time alone to visit so I took a walk and thought I'd take a peek at the new babies." Her cheeks pinked as if the admission embarrassed her. "I guess all of them except that little guy are with their mothers."

Neal looked through the glass at the infant swaddled in a blue blanket. "No, I think he's it. And baby Stacey, when she arrives. The nurses said they haven't had any babies in the past couple days."

Her eyes lit. "Emily's having her baby! It's a girl?"

"Yes and no. They don't know if it's a boy or a girl. Emily and Drew decided they'd rather be surprised. I automatically said she because the only babies I've had experience with are Emily and Autumn. I'm eight years older than Emily. So, I think *she* when I think of babies."

"Are your parents here, too? I haven't had a chance to talk with them since I moved back. I'd like to say hi."

"Not yet. Only me, and Drew now. He was still on his way home from New York when Emily went into labor. Mom and Dad weren't around, so I drove her. Drew arrived just in time to save me from getting dragged into being her substitute labor coach."

"Oh, but think of the experience." Her voice held a touch of awe.

"Not for me. Not again. Been there, done that."

Instead of the smile he expected, his words garnered a frown.

"You wouldn't have left her alone until Drew got here?"

"Of course not!" How could she even ask that? Emily was his little sister.

"I'm sorry. You sounded so adamant."

"No harm." He'd been joking around, although he couldn't say he wasn't majorly relieved when Drew showed up. If yesterday and today were any indication, Anne Howard no longer had Annie O'Connor's sense of humor. Somehow that saddened him.

"I'm going down to the cafeteria to get coffee. Would you like to join me?"

"No. Thanks. I'm going to go back to Edna's room." She paused, lips parted as if she was going to say more.

"You're sure?" Why was he pushing? The lady had already shot him down. The only answer he could come up with was that he missed the easy camaraderie they'd once shared as teens.

"No." She shook her head. "No coffee. I just wanted to tell you to check in with Professor Lawler on Monday. We've worked out an independent study program for you."

Neal stopped the crisp "Yes, ma'am" that was on the tip of his tongue. "Sure thing." He searched her eyes for any glimmer of personal interest, and his spirits plummeted when he saw none. "See you around."

As he descended the stairway, he resolved that when he talked to Jeff Lawler on Monday about the work study, he'd also ask him if he would be his advisor. The sooner he put some distance between him and Dr. Howard, the sooner he'd rid himself of his latent crush on Annie O'Connor.

Chapter Five

Neal wanted to switch academic advisors.

Anne reread the email Jeff Lawler had sent her late Monday. Her temper rose. This was the thanks she got after all she'd gone through to set up a work study assignment for him that would give him some meaningful engineering experience? Despite the juvenile stunt he'd pulled on her Friday?

Except Neal had no idea that she'd used her position as owner of Green Spaces Environmental Engineering, LLC to convince the birthing center project engineer to add Neal to his staff. Or that she'd said she'd supervise Neal, so the project engineer wouldn't be saddled with extra work. Her anger faded, leaving a hollow spot inside her. If Neal didn't want her as his academic advisor, how was he going to feel about spending ten hours a week working with her at the birthing center site?

She closed the email without responding and stared at her computer desktop.

Lord, what have I done? Didn't You put me here at NCCC to help older students like Neal and other disadvantaged students? To right some of the wrong Michael did when he embezzled from the scholarship fund the Green Spaces Engineering board of directors had set up?

Anne sat perfectly still, eyes shut, waiting for an answer that didn't come. She reached for the phone to call her friend Reenie. Reenie had introduced her to Jesus Christ when she was a lost college freshman, and had become Anne's refuge from the ping-pong relationship her feuding parents called a family. And she'd been there again for Anne after Michael had died, helping her find her way back to Him. She touched the phone and stopped. Reenie would be in class with her kindergarteners now.

She'd talk to her tonight. Besides, Anne knew what Reenie would say even without calling. That she was trying too hard. That all she needed to do was focus on the inner, and God would take care of the outer. As she rose and gathered her things for her Tuesday afternoon lecture, Anne said a small prayer of thanks that Reenie was always there to help her and vowed to do something in return.

The morning sun glinted off the metal construction office trailer that seemed to be standard issue for every commercial building site Neal had ever been to. He opened the door and stepped inside. "Hi, I'm Neal Hazard. I'm starting work here today."

The man seated at the desk frowned at Neal from behind his laptop computer.

"Jeff Lawler sent me. I have an orientation for my work study with Green Spaces at nine."

The other man stood, crossed the room and offered his hand. "I'm Gary Speer, the project manager. I was expecting someone…" He paused.

"Younger?" Neal asked.

"Yeah."

"I got a later start on college."

Gary cracked a half smile. "Take a seat. The engineer you'll be working with should be here anytime." He went back to his work.

Neal sat in the molded plastic chair Gary had pointed to. The fact that neither Jeff Lawler nor the project manager had mentioned the name of the engineer he'd be working with struck him as strange. But, since the project manager had more or less dismissed him, Neal refrained from interrupting the man's work to ask. He picked up a solar power company marketing brochure from the table next to the chair and read it, tapping his foot as the minutes clicked by on the wall clock.

Neal had hoped to get his orientation over in time to finish some electrical work at the campground that he hadn't gotten to Saturday. He'd been at the hospital most of the day. With his classes and other work, today looked like the best shot for getting the job done.

The door opened.

"Hi, sorry I'm late. I got caught behind a school bus."

Annie! Neal swallowed his surprise. Dressed as he hadn't seen her dressed since high school. She'd traded her usual tailored business wear for well-fitted jeans, a T-shirt, hooded sweatshirt and work boots.

What was she doing here? He'd talked with Jeff about changing advisors and had thought everything was cool. Maybe she was here as program director, even though she wasn't dressed the part.

"I'll clear out so that you can use the office," Gary said. "And I'll have those revised cost estimates to headquarters by the end of the week."

"Great. Everything else going smoothly?" Anne asked.

"As smooth as any job goes." Gary closed the laptop.

A sinking sensation started in Neal's chest and quickly dropped to his stomach. What was going on?

"Pull the chair up to the desk," she said as Gary left, "and we'll get started."

"*You're* the engineer I'll be working with?" His stomach knotted.

Her facial muscles tensed.

"I mean, I thought I'd be working with one of the Green Spaces engineers."

"You are."

The knot in his stomach loosened. "He'll be here soon?"

"You don't know?" Her voice trailed off.

"Know what?" Lately, he didn't seem to know much of anything. "Wait. You're doing consulting work with Green Spaces."

Heading up the environmental studies program at the college wasn't enough to keep her busy? He was having a hard enough time handling his relatively light class load and keeping his business going part-time.

"Sort of." She pressed her lips together as if debating what to say next. "I own Green Spaces."

Neal leaned forward, his eyes stormy. "You… own…Green Spaces Engineering?"

She backed up in her chair, buffeted by the heat radiating from him. "My husband, Michael, and I were partners." *In business, at least.* "I inherited his half when he died. I thought everyone knew."

"No, not everyone."

She wasn't sure why it mattered that she owned Green Spaces. But the challenge in his eyes, reminiscent of their Science Olympiad mental sparring, said it did.

"What does my position matter?"

His mouth opened and snapped shut.

She lifted her hand to reach over and touch his arm, as she'd so often done with Michael when he closed himself off because some action of hers had angered him.

"I guess it doesn't," he said in a strained voice.

She dropped her hand to her lap. "If you don't want to work with me, I could have Gary do it. I offered to take over the testing for the project so your work study wouldn't add to his workload. He's only scheduled to be here a couple weeks to get the permits set and the impact tests going. That's what you're going to be doing, helping me with the environmental impact tests. Construction will start in the spring."

As soon as the words had left her mouth, she knew she was being unfair. As much as it seemed that Neal didn't want to team up with her, unless he'd changed radically over the years, she knew he wouldn't want to impose on Gary. And, for reasons she didn't care to articulate even to herself, she wanted to personally introduce Neal to the hands-on work of environmental engineering, as Michael had introduced her. Although her late husband had failed her in other ways, he'd been a good mentor for her career.

Indecision shaded Neal's eyes. Maybe her memory wasn't serving her right. Maybe she didn't know Neal as well as she thought she did.

"Let's get started, then. I have a job scheduled for this afternoon."

Touché. He'd seen through her ploy, but hopefully no deeper to her inexplicable compulsion to see him excel in his college career.

"Come on. I'll show you around the site." She led him outside. "We're halfway between the Glen Falls Hospital and the Adirondack Medical Center in Saranac."

He quirked one side of his mouth up and jerked his head to the side in a gesture that said, "Tell me something I don't know."

She rushed on. "The site has five acres with a thousand feet of frontage on the road. It used to be part of a dairy farm." She bit her tongue. He probably knew that, too. "You can see where Gary and his crew have the building and parking lot marked off."

Neal nodded.

They walked around the perimeter of the future building.

"We'll be determining the impact of the construction and the operation of the facility on the local environment and community."

"Are you considering conservation measures to

reduce the energy costs to heat and cool the building?" Neal asked.

"We're building it to LEED standards with maximum insulation and triple pane thermal windows." She paused to gauge whether he was familiar with LEED, then plunged ahead with an explanation anyway. What was one more potentially duh statement? "LEED, that's Leadership in Energy and Environmental Design, an internationally recognized green building certification system."

"I'm familiar with it." The timbre of his voice changed. "Have you given any thought to solar voltaic power? Your project manager had some literature in the office."

"You're interested in PV?"

"Kind of. I am an electrician."

She hadn't thought of that. It did give him some expertise in that area. "Tell you what. I'll talk with Gary, and we'll make that the focus of your work study."

Neal looked at her, his expression inscrutable. She rocked on the balls of her feet.

"Fine with me," he said after an interminable couple of seconds.

That was it? No thanks for rejiggering the work study to suit his interests? But why should he? It wasn't like he'd asked her to change it. She had to stop trying to make her contact with Neal more than it was—an instructor supervising a student.

"You know that you'll be required to work ten hours a week."

"Yeah."

"Check your schedule and let me know what times are best for you."

"Will do."

At least she was getting a response now, sparse as it was. They completed the circle and approached the site office.

"For this week, you can look over the project proposal and the preliminary data on the energy demands it may create and start researching a solar power option."

She pushed her hair behind her ear. Was that relief she saw in his more relaxed stance?

"I have the building proposal in my case in the office, along with internet links to the local and state codes."

Neal kicked a rock out of their path with his work boot. "I appreciate what you're doing."

His belated thanks didn't bring any satisfaction. "I like to see students engaged in their work."

"I see." His toneless words mirrored her lack of inflection.

He reached around her for the door handle. She watched the play of his biceps as he opened the office door for her, and her mind flashed back to dancing in his strong arms at the mixer on Friday. It would be far too easy to let her relationship with

Neal become more than simply that of a teacher-mentor. Not that Neal had given her any indication he wanted anything more from her than a professional relationship. *Or even that,* she thought, remembering that he had requested Jeff replace her as his academic advisor.

He cleared his throat and Anne realized she was standing on the step blocking the door.

She moved into the office and across the room to Gary's desk where she'd left her case. "I'll get those plans and code books for you."

She removed the documents from her case and handed them to him. "Here you go."

"Thanks. I'll let you know about my schedule."

"Great, and if you have any questions, just ask."

"I don't now, but if I do, I'll get back to you."

He tapped the documents she'd given him against his thigh, reminding her that he'd said he had to get to a job. But she wasn't ready to let him go.

"I forgot to ask you…"

"What?" His brow creased and the tapping increased in tempo.

"Do you have a new niece or nephew?"

His features softened. "That's right. You weren't at church yesterday."

"No, I went to service at the Corner Stone Church in Ticonderoga. I'm still church shopping." Although by far, she'd liked the Hazardtown Community Church the best of the several she'd tried. "So tell me about the baby."

"It's a girl. Isabelle Genevieve Hazard Stacey. Eight pounds, two ounces. Twenty-two inches long."

"That's quite the name."

"Isabelle is because Jinx and Drew like it, Hazard—no hyphen—is to carry on the family name, and Genevieve is for my Grandma Hazard. She passed shortly after I came back from Afghanistan."

"I'm sorry. She lived in the big old house at the four corners where the new firehouse is now, right?"

"Yes, that's where the first Hazards had their trading post store. She and Grandpa sold it to the fire district when the old fire house burned down and bought a condo in Florida."

"It's sad to see property sold out of a family," Anne said, thinking of her own grandmother's house.

"We still have Lakeside."

"You and your sister plan to continue to run the campground when your father retires?"

"Jinx and I already own it in partnership with my parents." His rugged face beamed with boyish pride.

A partnership in the family campground, his electrician business and his return to college. Anne admired all that Neal had done with his life, despite the obstacles placed in his way. Or maybe because of them.

"Most of the property is rented to the Sonrise Camp and Convention Center, so there's not much to running it anymore, aside from renting out the big houses to the few families that come for vacation every year. The kids we played with when their parents vacationed here come with their families now."

Anne couldn't quell the jealousy stirred up inside her by the happy family picture Neal's words painted in her mind. She could barely imagine those kinds of deep family roots and connection to one place.

"Jinx and I had some great summers at the campground, even if she did try her best to get out of anything outdoors, especially if it involved work."

"Speaking of your sister," Anne said too brightly, "are she and Isabelle home? I have a little gift for the baby."

"They came home on Monday."

"Do you think Emily would mind if I stopped by and dropped it off later in the week?"

"No, not at all. She and Drew have an apartment in the lodge at the campground. Do you have her phone number?"

"No."

Neal reeled it off, and Anne punched the numbers into her cell phone.

"You might want to stop by and visit Mom, too. She mentioned that she didn't get to catch up with you at coffee hour the Sunday you came to the service at Community. She likes to be on top of what everyone is doing."

"I remember." What she remembered was that Mary Hazard had been interested in who Annie O'Connor was as a person—unlike her parents, who saw her as some kind of accomplishment to tout to friends.

"I'd better get going."

"I'll look for the email about your schedule."

She bit her lip and watched through the hazy trailer window as he drove off.

Neal caught up with his father at one of the campground cabins. "Hey, Dad. Starting without me?"

"No, making a graceful escape. Your mother and I came down to give Emily a hand. But the girl talk got too intense, so I decided it was time to leave."

Neal laughed. "I'm surprised Drew isn't here with you."

"He had some paperwork to catch up on in his office."

"Sure he did. You know Mom and Jinx probably did that on purpose to get rid of you guys."

"I couldn't have been married to your mother

for almost thirty-eight years and not have learned how to read her."

"Is that something you caught on to right away, or did it take time?" Neal placed his toolbox on the cabin floor and squatted to open it.

"It took a while."

Neal fiddled with the latch on the box, the hairs on his neck rising as he sensed his father's gaze on him.

"I hear from your sister that you're seeing an instructor at the college. Someone you know from high school."

Emily told Dad he was seeing Anne? Neal was hard-pressed to imagine how that topic had come up between his father and sister. Mom was the one who was concerned about his dating status.

"I'm not seeing Anne." He flipped the toolbox open with a bang.

"But you'd like to be."

He looked up at his father. "Did Mom put you up to this?"

His father snorted. "Your mother doesn't put me up to things."

Neal wasn't going to touch that statement with a ten-foot pole. He pulled the tool tray from the box and straightened to his full height. "Anne's supervising my work study."

"I suppose that could be a problem if you want it to be. Got twist caps in there?"

"Yes, Dad, I've done this a few times before." He shuffled his feet. "Anne owns Green Spaces Engineering."

"Isn't that the outfit from Boston that's putting up the new hospital in Ticonderoga?"

"The birthing center. Green Spaces is one of the biggest environmental engineering and consulting firms in the country."

"And?" his dad asked.

"I'm just an electrician." He studied the service wire coming into the cabin. His dad could have easily finished this job himself, except code required a licensed electrician to inspect the interior wiring and make the final hookup.

"Nothing wrong with that. And you're going to college."

Neal connected the service wire from the main lodge to the wiring his father had installed in the cabin and snapped the twist cap over the connection. "I'm not sure I'm cut out for college," he said to the wall.

"Not everyone is."

While Neal usually appreciated his father's habit of not giving advice unless asked, he wouldn't have minded a little more than the simple agreement Dad was offering.

"The only class I'm interested in is my work study." And that was going to require spending one-on-one time with Anne. He dropped the tool tray back in the box. "As part of it, I'm going to look at the possibilities of using solar power to reduce the energy costs of the center."

"Like the panel that runs the light at the state park boat launch?"

"But on a bigger scale. I wouldn't mind teaming up with the solar company to do the installation and maybe pick up some more work doing other installations."

"Sounds like a good opportunity to me. Take all you can from the work study and finish up the semester. Nothing says you have to go back next semester."

"If only it were that easy."

"Wait. You think this girl won't go out with you because you don't have a college degree?"

"It's got nothing to do with Anne."

"She's not worth it if she can't accept who you are," his dad said as if he hadn't spoken.

Neal snapped the toolbox cover shut. "How many cabins did you say are ready for hookups?"

"All ten."

"We'd better get to it, then." Neal picked up his tools and headed out the door.

"If it's eating at you that much," his father said to his retreating back, "you might want to give it up to God. Ask Him what He thinks."

Neal let the words roll over him. He'd been thinking of doing just that. The problem was he wasn't sure he was ready for His answer.

Chapter Six

"Hello," Mary Hazard called as she walked through the back door of the lodge into Emily and Drew's apartment.

"Out on the deck," Emily called back.

Mary placed the groceries on the counter and waved Anne through the kitchen to the living room.

She peered around Mary and through the screen door to the small crowd congregated on the deck. "It looks like they have company."

"No. Only family." Mary slid the screen open. "Look who I found at the Grand Union."

"Anne," Emily said. "Come out and join us. Drew has some steaks on the grill. We thought we'd eat out here."

Anne hovered by the door and scanned the group. There was Emily, Drew, Emily's father, Ted, Autumn, a young man who must be her boyfriend—and Neal, leaning against the deck rail with a bemused expression on his face. She lifted her hand to her head to make sure she didn't have a maple leaf or something stuck in her hair.

"You're having dinner. I don't want to intrude. I have a little gift for Isabelle. I'll just drop it off and be on my way." *Back to Grandma's too quiet, empty house.*

"You're not intruding," Mary said. "Sit down. You're welcome to stay for dinner."

Emily's husband, Drew, unfolded a lawn chair at the head of the picnic table. "There you go."

"Okay. But I can only stay for a few minutes." Anne handed a small wrapped package to Emily.

Emily took the gift. "You shouldn't have, but we'll take it." She grinned and tore the wrapping off.

"They're onesies," Anne explained. "My friend Reenie said she couldn't get enough of them when her son, my godson, Ian, was an infant."

Emily ripped open the plastic package and held the little garment with pink and blue bunnies up in front of Isabelle. The infant squirmed in the baby seat on the table, rubbed her eyes and yawned.

"She loves it," Emily said.

"Really," Neal drawled. "And here I thought she was getting sleepy."

Emily placed the onesie in her lap and picked up the other one with yellow and green bears. "Obviously, you've had far fewer conversations with

Izzie than I have. If she were sleepy, she would have yawned first before rubbing her eyes."

"Is she serious?" Neal asked his brother-in-law.

"Dead serious. I'm still learning baby. I often have Em translate for me."

"It's girl baby, bro. We may never be fluent."

"True."

"Stop," Emily ordered. "And get back to grilling my dinner. I'm starved."

"You've been starved since you found out we were expecting Isabelle." Drew gave his wife a loving perusal that expanded to include his daughter.

Anne settled and resettled herself in the lawn chair and picked at a rough spot in her fingernail as she struggled to control the intense craving to belong that the easy banter raised.

"What can I say? This eating for two is tough."

Neal pushed away from the railing. "Can't have you wasting away in front of our eyes. Did you get the salsa and chips, Mom?"

"They're on the counter in the kitchen."

"You're staying, Anne?" he asked.

She jerked her head up. Was he offering a real invitation? Her pulse quickened. His open expression said yes. But, after his standoffish demeanor this morning, she suspected he was simply politely extending his mother's invitation.

"Of course she's staying. Go get the chips." His

mother waved him into the house. "You don't have other plans, do you?"

A perfect opportunity to beg off. Except she didn't have anywhere else to go. "No, I'm free."

"Good. We have plenty." Mary sat on the edge of the picnic table bench. "Autumn made a potato salad. It's her specialty."

"Because it's my favorite and, if I don't make it, no one else will."

"Poor deprived baby," Emily said.

Autumn good-naturedly stuck her tongue out at her aunt.

Anne tensed, waiting for Mary to reprimand her granddaughter for her "unladylike behavior" as Anne's mother would have done to her.

Mary ignored them both. "I picked up the fixings for a tossed salad. Autumn, will you run in and see what's taking your father so long?"

"Sure." She left with her friend trailing after her and returned a couple of minutes later with the salsa and chips.

"Food," Emily said as she scooped up salsa with a tortilla chip and popped it in her mouth.

Autumn and her friend sat on the picnic bench across the table from Emily. "Dad's making the salad."

"Good. As soon as the steaks are done, we'll be set." Mary slid the screen door open for Neal, who carried a large wooden salad bowl in one hand and a place setting in the other.

He put the salad on the table and the plate and flatware in front of Anne before he sat on the picnic bench to her right.

"Steaks are done." Drew carried a large platter to the table and sat next to his wife.

Mary and Ted took their seats.

"Autumm, would you say the blessing?" her grandfather asked.

Emily reached for Anne's left hand and Neal for her right one. His fingers were warm and his grip strong. Anne closed her eyes and bowed her head, silently chiding herself for noticing.

"Bless this food to our use, and us to thy service. Fill our hearts with grateful praise. Amen," Autumn finished.

Emily and Neal released Anne's hands. She dropped her right hand to her lap and flexed her fingers. What was with her? It wasn't as if she'd never held a man's hand in prayer.

"Guests first," Mary said. "Anne, pass your plate to Drew."

Drew placed a steak on the plate, passed it back and then served the others. The meal passed quickly in a torrent of friendly chatter. When everyone had finished, Mary stood and picked up her and Ted's plates.

"Can I do anything to help?" Anne asked.

"Yes," Emily chimed in ahead of her mother. "You can come and keep me company while I change Izzie."

Isabelle seconded her mother's invitation with a loud wail.

"Yes, I know." Emily picked up her daughter and comforted her. "This way."

She led Anne back into the lodge to a small bedroom off the living room. The view out of the window showcased the campground's pine forest that seemed to go on forever.

"It's so quiet and serene here."

"For now, except for this imp." Emily placed Isabelle on her Winnie the Pooh changing table. "Summers when camp is in session are something else. We had five hundred campers this year."

Anne watched in admiration while Emily changed Isabelle with an expertise that belied her new motherhood. "You make that look so easy." Anne's own experience with diapers the couple of times she'd babysat Ian for Reenie had gone nowhere near as smoothly.

"I get lots of practice, and I babysat when I was in high school. You should see Autumn. She's as good or better at this than I am." Emily picked up Isabelle and patted her on her freshly diapered bottom.

The way Emily naturally responded to her daughter as if it were second nature tugged at Anne's heartstrings. She'd never had a chance to babysit, except for Reenie. She and her parents had moved around so much, and when they did settle in somewhere, her parents put the neighbors off with their incessant arguing. So, no one ever asked her to watch their children.

"You work at the campground with Drew?" Emily's use of *we* when she'd referred to the campers seemed to say so. "For some reason, I thought you were a graphic artist."

"I am. Do you mind holding her while I clean up here?" Without waiting for an answer, Emily handed off Isabelle to Anne.

She held her stiffly, arms extended for a moment before cradling the infant against her as Emily had. Isabelle burrowed her little face into Anne's shoulder, and Anne relaxed, breathing in the soothing smells of baby powder and lotion.

Emily disposed of the diaper, used a baby wipe to clean her hands and the changing table and tossed the wipe in the wastebasket. "That takes care of that."

At the sound of her mother's voice, Isabelle squirmed and began to fuss, clutching at Anne's blouse with her tiny hands. She patted the baby's back and her fussing turned into a full-fledge cry. Helplessness filled Anne.

"Come here." Emily lifted her daughter from Anne's arms. "Is that any way to treat our company?"

Isabelle's cry subsided to a wimper.

"She's hungry. Do you mind?" Emily grabbed a receiving blanket from the compartment under the changing table and motioned to two matching rocking chairs next to the window.

"No, of course not. But I can go if you'd like some privacy."

"Oh, no. Stay." Emily sat in one of the rocking chairs and settled Isabelle in. "I get plenty of privacy. Summer camp may be over but Drew still has a lot of planning to do for next year, and the conference center has events year-round. He may work at home, but that doesn't mean we see him any more often than if his office were in town instead of downstairs. What I could use is some company, girl company."

"Okay." Anne joined her in the other rocking chair.

"You asked me about my work."

Work. Anne was much more comfortable with that subject. She leaned back against the chair's wooden back.

"I'm not a camp employee. Dad and Drew are the only ones who work for the coalition of churches that sponsors the camp. Dad handles maintenance. The rest of us just hang around and help with whatever."

"It's nice that you can depend on each other like that." The only thing Anne could depend on from her parents was criticism of her and each other.

Emily shrugged, jostling Isabelle, who made a small protest before resuming her nursing. "Neal and I grew up helping Mom and Dad with the campground. Back then, we rented sites to families and other vacationers, along with the three big cabins we still rent out. I can't say that I was a joyful helper. I wasn't much of an outdoor kid."

"I've never been camping, but I went to Y camp one summer." Anne tamped down the conflicting memories of the great time she'd had and her disappointment the next summer when her parents, in a rare moment of solidarity, had decided her summers would be better spent in more educational summer programs. "I suppose being a camper is a lot different than keeping up a campground, and I know how it is when parents think you should like things you don't."

"No, I was a brat. Neal loved working at the campground, so I thought he should do it all. My parents had other ideas like teaching me responsibility, respect and a strong work ethic—things I appreciate now and am planning to do with my kids. And, somehow, despite not getting my way and spending summers sitting on the deck sketching, I was still able to become a graphic artist."

"Kids, plural?" As an only child who'd often wished for siblings, Anne warmed more toward Emily. Because of career demands, many of Anne's collegues were choosing to have only one child. "You and Drew plan on having more?"

"God willing. Of course, Drew would like to have a boy."

"Men. Wouldn't they all." Anne suspected that one of the reasons Michael had kept putting off their having children was because he already had the two boys from his first marriage.

"Not all of them. Neal insists that Autumn is enough for him. Sometimes I think he's serious, which would be a shame. He's a great dad, and I'm not saying that because he's my brother. You've met Autumn."

Anne laughed. "You could be a little prejudiced there, too." But she wasn't. From what Anne had seen and heard about Autumn at NCCC, she was an admirable young woman. And Neal's love for and pride in his daughter were evident to all. It wasn't hard for Anne to imagine him raising another child, to picture a miniature version of Neal, shadowing him, trying to do everything just like Dad.

Emily resettled her now-sleeping daughter. "I think the right woman could change his mind." She looked directly at Anne.

Her throat clogged. Emily couldn't mean her. She couldn't convince a husband who insisted that he wanted children with her when the time was right to commit to having a child. How could she be the woman to convince Neal, who professed to not want any more children? She glanced down at the sleeping Isabelle. And Neal's children would be beautiful. Autumn was.

Footsteps sounded on the pine plank flooring outside Isabelle's nursery, followed by a knock. Anne shook off her nonsensical thoughts of her and Neal and children as the door opened wide.

"Talking about me again, Jinx?"

"And what would make you think that, aside from an inflated ego?"

"As soon as you heard me coming—silence." He really hadn't thought they were talking about him. He'd just wanted to burst in on his sister. But the pink tinge on Anne's cheeks said they had been. He grinned in reaction while he waited for his sister's comeback.

"How would we have known it was you?"

"You certainly must know Drew's footsteps, Mom would have been quieter and Dad would have sent Mom." He crossed his arms and waited for Em's retort.

"While all true, I hate to break this to you, but you're not the center of everyone's attention."

"Then, you weren't talking about me?"

Emily smoothed Isabelle's baby fuzz back from her forehead. "What's brought you to our humble presence?"

Neal glanced from his sister to Anne and secretly gloated. They had been talking about him. If they hadn't Emily would have said so. She wouldn't come out and lie about it, so she'd evaded the question. And he wasn't going to lie to himself. He wouldn't mind being the center of Anne's attention. She was a beautiful, talented woman.

"We thought we'd go get soft-serve ice cream."

"What's the occasion?" Emily asked.

"You have to have an occasion to have soft-serve?" Anne asked.

"It's a family thing."

Emily might have missed the light fading in Anne's eyes, but Neal didn't.

She dropped her gaze to her wristwatch. "It's going on seven-thirty. I should get going. I have papers to grade tonight."

"Emily doesn't mean it's for family only," Neal added.

"Of course not." Emily backed him up. "I only meant that we go out for soft-serve ice cream to celebrate family occasions." She raised her hand in front of her. "Don't tell me. Autumn and Jack have been acting funny. Are they—"

"Don't even think it. They aren't engaged." He

had trouble keeping the outrage he felt out of his voice. "She's only nineteen and not done with college yet." And he certainly wasn't ready to have his only child truly be an adult yet. Not by a long shot.

Emily countered him. "And how did you know that's what I was going to say?"

He made himself relax. Emily always challenged him. She always had. "Great minds and all that. And I've noticed them acting funny, too."

Emily turned to Anne as if she'd just noticed the other woman was still there. "Sorry about all the family talk."

"No need to apologize." The way she held her fists clenched in her lap was in direct contrast to the almost bemused expression on her face.

It hit him. She thought he and Emily were arguing or an argument was going to break out. He hadn't been around her family much as a teen, but knew they had a different and more volatile relationship than the God-based one he and his family had.

"What we're celebrating is…" His voice sounded more like an over-eager TV game show host than the upbeat tone he wanted.

"Give me one more guess. Your return to college. We haven't celebrated that yet."

Neal studied the knot in the pine plank in front of his right foot. The jury was still out on whether that was any cause to celebrate, except maybe for his work study with Green Spaces, and he wasn't one hundred percent sure about that. Things could be tense with Anne supervising him.

"No."

Anne flinched. He hadn't realized he'd raised his voice. He stepped toward her to touch her shoulder in reassurance, but stopped when he saw the speculative look on his sister's face. Anne seemed fine now. Maybe he imagined the flinch. No sense giving Emily anything to fuel the matchmaking tendency she'd developed since she and Drew had gotten together. She was possibly worse than his mother, who'd been encouraging him to date for years.

He dropped his raised hand. "What we're celebrating, dear sister, is the arrival of Isabelle."

"Oh." She beamed. "That *is* something to celebrate."

As if to give her approval, Isabelle woke up, stretched and favored her uncle with a big drooly smile.

Neal melted. And by the goofy grin on Anne's face, the effect was universal. No denying his niece was a cutie. He thought she looked a lot like Autumn in that smushy-faced newborn way.

"It's settled, then. Everyone else is ready when you are."

"I'll check her to see if she needs another change and be right out. Anne?"

Anne touched her lips with her finger. "No, it's a family outing. I was only going to come in and drop off the gift, and I've already stayed for dinner."

Emily stood and lifted Isabelle to her shoulder. "We'd be more than happy to have you come."

Anne lifted her gaze to Neal. He stepped back. "Yeah, we'd like you to come."

"No, but thank you. I have those papers waiting at home."

Emily glared at him.

What had he done? He'd invited Anne just like he'd invited her for coffee the other day at the hospital. She'd declined then and she'd declined now. And, when he thought about it, like Anne had said, it was a family occasion. Anne and everyone else would get to celebrate with them at Isabelle's baptism.

"I'll go say bye to your folks."

"If you insist," Emily said. "Thanks again for the gift. Will we see you Sunday at church?"

"You're welcome, and you might. I want to visit your church again before I make a decision." Anne turned toward the door.

"I'll walk you out."

"No need." She stepped into the living room.

"What?" he asked as soon as Anne was out of earshot and before his sister could reprimand him.

"If you don't know, my telling you won't help."

Emily was real helpful. But he was afraid he did

know. It had something to do with Anne not being family but him wanting her to come with them anyway. And he was fairly sure that the reason behind that feeling was one of those answers to his prayers that he didn't want to hear.

Chapter Seven

Anne studied her reflection in the bedroom mirror. Despite their prewashed finish, her jeans shouted brand-new, and the pale blue hoodie that had looked so cute and casual on the rack at the mall in Queensbury last Saturday looked too cute and not casual enough today. She should have picked up a real sweatshirt at the Paradox Lake General Store. Fieldwork was business. It didn't call for cute. She tore off the hoodie and tossed it on the bed. Maybe her long-sleeved T-shirt would be enough. But the early frost glistening on the grass outside her window cancelled that idea.

What was wrong with her? She'd done hundreds of site inspections before without going through any clothing trauma. *But not site inspections with Neal Hazard,* a little voice in her head pointed out. She hated when her little voice was right. Dinner at the Hazards' last Friday and the feelings dredged up by her after-dinner conversation with Emily had set her on edge the whole week.

She'd gone to services at a church in Schroon Lake, rather than the Hazardtown Community Church as she'd planned, telling herself it was because she needed to visit all of the churches on her list before going back to any of the ones she'd already visited, not to avoid Neal and his family. The minute she'd walked in the other church she'd realized she didn't belong there. She was fighting God's will again, staying away from the one church in the area she'd found a spiritual connection to because…why? Because the Hazards were a happy family and she wanted to be a part of that but couldn't be?

Anne yanked the hoodie back on. She wasn't that lost little girl anymore. She was a successful woman. A business owner. A college professor. She zipped up the sweatshirt. The head of a college program. Someone who was in control of her life. The breath she'd been holding whooshed out. And the woman who'd studiously avoided Neal *and* his daughter at the college all week.

But not today. Anne glanced at her alarm clock. In twenty minutes, she was meeting Neal at the birthing center site to conduct a solar site analysis. *Correct that.* To show him how to conduct an analysis, as his instructor. She spun away from the mirror and went downstairs to collect her equipment.

* * *

Neal grabbed a travel mug of coffee on his way through the kitchen and slammed a top on it. He had fifteen minutes to make the twenty-five-minute drive to Ticonderoga to meet Anne. He should have known he didn't have time to pound out his outline for his English composition class this morning. But he'd been dead tired when he'd gotten home from the not-so-quick-as-he'd-expected wiring inspection he'd scheduled for yesterday evening.

The job hadn't passed his inspection, and he'd felt badly for the young couple who were finishing the second floor of their house themselves. They needed a second bedroom for the imminent arrival of their first child. Neal had stayed and showed them what needed to be done to bring the wiring up to code and scheduled another inspection for next week. No way he had the energy to tackle his homework after he'd gotten home.

His cell phone rang as he reached for the door handle of his pickup. His breath caught. Anne calling to cancel? He hadn't seen her all week, wondered if she was purposely avoiding him because he'd somehow driven her off, according to Emily, with his invitation to go for ice cream. But Anne was too professional for that and had confirmed they were on for this morning when he'd emailed her on Tuesday. He fumbled in his pocket for his phone, popping the top off the mug and almost giving himself a coffee shower when he hit it against the truck door.

It wasn't Anne. It was Autumn. "Hi, what's up?" he asked.

"My car won't start, and I'm supposed to be at the medical center for my clinical shift at ten. It's probably the battery again. Can you come over and give me a jump? Jule had an early class today, and Jack's out on a tow job on the Northway. I *can't* be late." Her words tumbled out in a long breathless stream.

"I'll be right there."

"Thanks. What would I do without you? Bye."

Neal whistled as he checked the tool chest in the bed of his truck to make sure he had jumper cables. The bright morning sun reflected off the silver bed lining. It was good to know Autumn still needed him, even if it was only occasionally and happened to be an inconvenience today.

Before he put his phone away, he tried Anne's number to tell her he'd be late. His call went right to her voice mail. She was probably in one of the many local dead zones. He left a voice message and a text message for good measure.

Autumn was pacing her driveway when he arrived. He pulled his truck up to face her car and got out.

"I backed in last night in case I needed a jump this morning. I've been having so much trouble with it."

"Could be you need a new battery," he couldn't stop himself from pointing out.

She sighed. "That's what Jack said, too. But I was waiting until I got paid tomorrow at the nursing home so I wouldn't have to hit you up for the money."

He dropped his arm around her shoulders. "I appreciate that, but you have a long drive to the hospital for your classes. Your car needs to be working. So, let's see what I can do. Open the hood. I'll get my jumper cables."

Neal fastened the cables to the battery in Autumn's car and his truck battery and turned the truck on. "All set. Hop in and give it a try."

Autumn climbed in her car and turned the key. It responded with one grinding whine and then just clicked.

"Shut it off." Neal turned the truck off, checked the cables and turned it on again. "Give it another try."

Autumn turned the key and all she got was more clicks.

"Stop. It's dead."

"But I have to get to the hospital."

He unfastened the cable from the truck and the car and removed the car battery. "You can use the pickup."

"Thanks, Dad. You're the best." She scrambled

from the car and gave him a hug. "I'd better call in. By the time I drive you home and back, I'll be late."

"You don't have to drive me home." He closed the car hood. "I'm supposed to be meeting Anne at the work site." He checked his watch. "About a half hour ago. You can drop me off on your way."

"I'm sorry. I made you late."

"No problem." At least he hoped it wasn't a problem. He had the whole morning free, but that didn't mean Anne did.

He hoisted the car battery into the back of the pickup and pulled his wallet from his pocket as he walked around to the cab door. Autumn was already in the driver's seat. He handed her a credit card. "Pick a battery up on your way home from the hospital. You should be able to turn the old one in for credit toward the new one."

"Thanks. Jack can put it in for me. I'll pay you back after I pick up my check."

He shook his head. "It's on me."

"Wait. How will you get home?"

"I'll see if Anne can give me a lift and, if not, I'll call your grandfather."

"Just like me. Calling Dad to the rescue."

Neal gritted his teeth. She was teasing, but he hadn't thought of it like that. "We'd better get a move on if you don't want to be late." He resisted a strong urge to grab the assist handle above the door. He wasn't used to being in the passenger seat.

A couple of minutes later, Autumn pulled into the birthing center site.

"You can drop me here. I'll walk back to the office."

"Thanks again. I'll bring the truck right home. I don't have any classes this afternoon."

"That's fine." He waved her off and trudged up the dirt road. Anne opened the office door as he reached the site trailer.

"Hi. I'd about given up on you. I did say nine o'clock, didn't I?" The sun passed behind a cloud throwing a gray shadow on Anne and the trailer.

"Yes," he said, feeling every bit the chastised student he was. "Autumm had car trouble. I had to stop on the way and help her." No need to mention that he'd already been late before his daughter had called and delayed him more. "She dropped me off at the road and I walked up."

Anne looked out past him. "So that's why I didn't hear you pull in."

Neal noticed she had her briefcase. She must have been leaving. He wasn't that late, not more than thirty, maybe forty minutes. But, then, in their high school days, Anne had always been punctual.

"I tried to call, but couldn't get through."

"Come on in."

She walked to the table at the back of the office. He nodded and stepped over beside her.

"I tried to reach you, too, but I don't have any

service bars here. These are the report forms we have to fill out for Gary." Anne handed him a clipboard from the table. "I've already sent him all of the code information you included in your research. Good job, by the way."

The sincere smile she gave him didn't quite wipe out the dig of her "good job" comment. To him, it sounded like something Autumn's pre-school teacher would have said. Did say, in fact. All the time. He flipped through the report pages on the clipboard. What was with him today? Anne wouldn't have said "good job" if she didn't mean it.

"Thanks."

"Let's go out and get started on the evaluation."

Neal opened the door for Anne and followed her out. The breeze carried the light floral fragrance he was beginning to think of as Anne's scent mingled with mountain pine.

"I'm going to put my case in the car. Can you lock the office?"

He met her in front of her car, and she showed him the solar meter she'd picked up from the passenger seat. She slipped another meter into the pocket of her hoodie.

"We need to go over to the building site and take measurements at several spots to see where the sun is most direct." She lifted her head and surveyed the sky. "Although it looks like we're losing the sun."

"The wind has picked up, too. Looks like a storm is moving in. Is there enough sun for us to get accurate readings?" He thought there was, but she was the engineer.

"As long as the storm doesn't move in too fast." She strode over to the far right corner of the mapped-out building position. "I'll show you how to use the meter by taking the first reading. You can write down my numbers on the report. Then, you can take the rest of them."

Neal leaned forward, eyes fixed on the meter and watched and listened as Anne explained and took the readings. He wouldn't mind if all his classes were like this, casual atmosphere, lovely teacher presenting information he could see as useful.

"Got it." She rattled off the last number and he wrote it down. "Ready to do the next one?"

"Ready." She handed him the meter and he reset it to zero as she'd showed him.

"We need to take the next reading at the halfway point between this corner and the far corner." She pulled the other device from her pocket. "Pace it out. The building dimensions are on the site map on the last sheet, behind the report pages."

"Is that a digital laser measure?"

Her eyes brightened. "Yes. Have you used one before?"

"No, I've only read about them."

"They're really cool. I'll show you."

He stepped closer.

"See the pine tree at the far edge of the site before the ground slopes down?"

"Uh-huh."

"Watch." She held the meter and punched the buttons. "See?" She turned the meter to him and rocked forward, her every move radiating enthusiasm.

This was Annie, the science nerd he remembered so well from high school.

He read the measurement. "Are they as accurate as they say they are?"

"You tell me." She stepped back until her toes touched the stake delineating the close corner of the proposed building and shot a measurement to the far corner. "Now, read me the dimensions of the building from the site map."

Neal obliged.

She flashed the meter in his face. He grabbed it, brushing the soft skin of her hand with his callused fingers, and whistled. "Down to the sixteenth."

"Told you it was cool."

"Can I try it?"

"Sure. Shoot the distance to the office." Anne placed her left hand on his forearm and pointed directions with her right.

As Neal sighted the meter, a clap of thunder sounded in the distance. Anne's grip on his arm tightened and threw the laser off mark.

"Sorry, try again." She dropped her hand and held it clenched at her side.

Anne was afraid of thunderstorms? Neal shrugged off her reaction, sighted the meter again and took a reading. He turned to show it to Anne. Her eyes were focused at the dark bank of clouds moving in. She took a deep breath. "Let's pace off the distance to the trailer. The storm is moving in. You'll have to finish the solar evaluation another day."

"Sure." Although from the threatening look of the sky, they might want to move faster than a pace. He was convinced the laser meter was accurate.

"My stride is twenty-six inches."

For some reason, it didn't surprise him that Anne knew that.

She started toward the office methodically counting her paces, her jaw set and mouth drawn in a thin line. Another crack of thunder sounded closer. She faltered and her lips parted as if she were talking to herself before resuming her count.

"You don't have to do that. I saw how right on the meter was when we took the building measurement."

Lightning flashed across the now-dark sky. He waited for the thunder and Anne's reaction.

"Yes, I do." Her movement was almost trancelike.

The expected boom came and with it a deluge of rain.

"No, you don't." Neal grabbed her hand and pulled her after him to her parked car. The passenger-side door was closest. He breathed a sigh of relief when it opened and she climbed in without protest. He raced around the car to the other door, not that he wasn't already drenched.

Once he was seated behind the wheel, Anne looked at him wide-eyed. "I don't like thunderstorms."

That seemed like an understatement.

"You don't have to drive me home. I'm okay— really. You can go. Here, take the solar meter." She shoved it at him. "You can come back and take the readings later in the week, whenever you have time."

"I don't have my truck. Autumn took it to Saranac." He hoped the storm would let up before his daughter had to drive back.

"Oh, that's right." She studied her hands clenched in her lap. "I can give you a lift home. I don't have any classes until this afternoon."

"I'd appreciate that. But why don't I drive to my place? By then, the storm should let up some."

She opened her mouth.

"I know you're perfectly capable of driving in the rain. Humor me. I don't like to ride with other people."

"All right." She unclenched her hands and dug in her jeans pocket for the car keys.

The storm fired off three more claps of thunder with no pause between. Anne made a strangled sound and dropped the keys she was handing to Neal. He caught them and her hand as she tried to save them from falling.

"Like you said, you don't like storms." He held on to her hand and let the keys drop to his lap.

She pulled her hand from his and crossed her arms. "It's a kid thing." She unfolded her arms and raised her hands, palms forward, shaking her head. "I should be past it."

He picked up the key and put it in the ignition. "But you're not. We all have stuff like that." He turned the key, put the car in Drive and started down the dirt road to the highway.

"It's stupid. Dad was teaching me not to fear storms. There's nothing to be afraid of."

She said the last words as if they were an affirmation.

Lightning flashed close in front of them. He half expected her to repeat *there's nothing to be afraid of.* Neal glanced over. Her eyes were squeezed shut.

"I was about three or four. It was a bad storm. Like this one. I was crying because the noise scared me."

Neal shifted in his seat and scratched a sudden itch on the back of his neck.

"He took me to my room, threw open the curtains and explained that the storm showed us God's power and glory, and locked me in."

Neal swallowed hard. He hadn't been much impressed with the glimpses he'd gotten of her parents when he and Anne were teens. That impression dropped about one hundred points. What was the guy thinking, saying that to a little girl? God was a loving father. At least the God Neal knew. He wouldn't use his awesome power to frighten small children.

"I never cried during a storm again." She looked over at him as if she'd just realized he was there. "I'm sorry. Too much information. I'm fine."

Sure, if you didn't count her chalk-white pallor and the way she sat rigid against the back of the seat, her feet flat on the floor.

He shrugged it off. "It's okay." Before he could decide whether to say anything more, a bolt of lightning streaked across the sky so close he blinked from the flash. The resounding thunder was deafening.

"That was a close one." He wanted to take the words back as soon as they left his mouth.

Anne released a strangled screech and, out of the corner of his eye, Neal caught motion to the right. Almost as if in slow motion, one of the towering pine trees bent and then plummeted across the road ahead. He slammed on the brakes and felt the car skid forward on the mud.

Lord, help me.

Gripping the wheel as hard as he could, he turned into the slide. His experience driving on icy, snow-covered roads paid off. The car came to a halt parallel to the fallen tree.

Heart pounding, he looked up at the angry gray sky. "Thank You," he mouthed before turning toward Anne. "Are you…"

She sat perfectly still, not making a sound, eyes scrunched shut and tears streaming down her cheeks. He gathered her into his arms and pressed her head against his shoulder. Her hair was soft and damp against his hand. "It's okay. We didn't hit it."

She burst into loud sobs, gulping for air. He rubbed her back and tried to soothe her as he'd done with Autumn when she was frightened as a child. But Anne was no child and the protective feelings he was experiencing weren't those of a father toward his child. How could Anne's father have done that to her?

Anne shuddered and breathed deeply, bringing her sobs under control. "I'm sorry."

He held her close for another moment before allowing her to push away.

"I don't know what got into me, breaking down like that." She straightened and smoothed her hair.

He caught her hand as she dropped it to her lap and rubbed it with his thumb. "It's okay. I find large trees crashing to the ground in front of my car on the scary side, too." The smile he'd hoped to coax out of her didn't come.

"No."

"Crashing trees aren't scary?"

"No. Yes." One corner of her mouth curved up.

"That's my girl."

She tilted her head and stared at him for a second, her brow furrowed.

"No, the storm. I don't lose control like that. Not like that." Her voice trailed off and she looked out the side window away from him.

He wanted to draw her back into his arms and comfort her, let her know it was all right to be afraid sometimes. But he knew better. The set of her shoulders told him the self-controlled college professor was returning.

"No sense sitting here. We should go back to the trailer and wait out the storm. Once it lets up, we can walk into Ticonderoga, and I can call someone about getting the tree removed so we can get your car out. I should be able to get cell reception there."

Anne shook her head. She had to get away from here and Neal. The embarrassment was too much. "There's another way out. The driveway to the house that used to be on the property goes to a side road that you can take to the highway. You'll need to turn around and drive past the trailer."

Neal rocked the car back and forth, tires spinning, until they caught traction. He turned around and drove back past the office. She ignored the muscle working in his jaw. He had every right to be impatient with her and her childish behavior.

"See ahead, the road curves to the left? That's the old driveway."

Neal relaxed his steel-eyed attention to the road long enough for a quick nod.

The rain pelted the windshield in blinding sheets. She bit her lip as she felt the car slip in the mud again, or thought she felt it slip. Neal kept his hands straight on the wheel. So she must have imagined it. The pounding of her heart slowed and she released her lip when the tires crunched on the stone of the old driveway.

Neal turned left when they reached the highway.

"The lake's the other way," she said.

"I know. I'm going to take you to the college. You don't want to be driving back from the lake in this weather and you said you had classes this afternoon."

Relief loosened the band of fear constricting her chest, followed by guilt about leaving Neal stranded at NCCC and a twinge of embarrassment that he was playing white knight saving her from the storm. Escaping to her office, rather than spending another twenty minutes in her car making polite conversation sounded very inviting. Whatever had possessed her to share that stupid story about her dad and thunderstorms?

"That's fine for me, but how will you get home?"

"I'll get a hold of Autumn and have her swing by and pick me up when she's done at the hospital. I have some classwork I can do in the computer lab."

"If you're sure." She hoped her voice didn't sound as cheery to him as it did to her. Storms usually didn't get to her like the one today had, not anymore. She would have been fine without Neal's comforting, given a minute or two. Still it had been nice to have his strong arms around her when the storm was crashing around them.

"Are you okay?"

"What? Fine. Why?"

"You were so still. I thought maybe the storm…"

"No. I'm good. I was thinking. Getting in early would be good. I've got a lot of things I can catch up on before my class this afternoon." And in her office, she could shut out the storm with the window blinds, and the lingering thoughts of Neal holding her.

She ignored the puzzled look he shot her. Letting him get close to her wasn't an option. He was her student. Besides, his comforting her about the storm was simply his paternal instinct reacting to her juvenile fear. She was an adult, not the teenaged girl who'd had a crush on Neal Hazard that she'd denied to everyone, including herself. Reading any more into his action would be as childish as her fear.

Chapter Eight

"Smooth, Hazard." Tyler from his English composition class caught up with Neal in the hall as he approached Anne's office.

"Tyler," Neal said, slowing his pace.

"Ryan saw you and Professor Howard pulling into the parking lot in her car the other morning."

Neal gripped the metal binder he'd been carrying casually at his side until it almost cut into his fingers. "We were out at the new birthing center building site doing a solar site analysis for my independent study."

"Independent study. Sure, if that's what you want to call it. You didn't happen to notice there was a thunderstorm?"

Neal repeated the Lord's commandment *Love thy neighbor as thyself* to himself as struggled not to wipe the smirk off the guy's face. On second thought, maybe he didn't love himself that much today.

"Don't talk about her like that."

"Back off. I was complimenting you."

"You weren't complimenting the lady."

The corner of Tyler's mouth twisted and his eyes narrowed as if he didn't understand.

"Hey, Dad! Glad I caught you." Autumn waved as she stepped out of a classroom across the hall.

Tyler's eyes widened. "That's your daughter?"

"Yeah." He'd better not be getting any ideas about Autumn.

"Uh, I didn't know you were *that* old. I thought you were my brother's age, like twenty-six or seven. Sorry if I offended."

Neal would have laughed if he weren't still steamed about the assumptions Tyler had made about Anne and him. She probably wouldn't like him stepping in on her behalf, but gossip about her and a student wouldn't be good. Better he quash the buzz before it got back to Anne.

"See you around."

"Right, and watch what you're saying about people." Neal used his best imitation of his National Guard commander.

Tyler was gone before Autumn had crossed the hall to Neal.

"What was that?" she asked.

"You don't want to know. What's up?"

"Professor Murray stopped me on my way out of my Irish literature class. She's been trying to get ahold of you. She said she's sent you several emails."

"I don't check my school account that often. It's a pain to have to log into the computer, rather than being able to check the messages on my phone."

"You're not having trouble with her class, are you?"

He was. But he wasn't about to tell Autumn that. "English never was my strongest subject." But he'd never done as poorly as he seemed to be doing in his composition class. He'd gotten a C on his how-to paper on installing a light fixture. The instructor had said to write about something they knew. Then, when she'd graded his paper, she'd said it was too technical, that an average person wouldn't be able to follow it. Neal had wanted to challenge her, but had let it drop. And Tyler whooping about how he'd gotten an A with his how-to-pick-up-women paper hadn't helped.

"She probably wants you to come in so she can go over your paper with you."

He hadn't said anything about his paper.

"I had her last year."

"And if I remember correctly, you got an A."

"Yeah, I aced the class, but Jule had trouble with her first couple of papers."

"I didn't say I was having trouble."

Autumn quirked an eyebrow. "Well, if you do, maybe I can give you a hand."

"Sure thing." The last thing he needed was his daughter tutoring him. "I've got to get going." He raised his binder. "Anne's waiting for these solar readings I took yesterday."

Amusement lit Autumm's eyes. "You couldn't have emailed them?"

"Don't get smart with me." His chuckle took the edge off his words. She *was* smart, as smart or smarter than he'd been at her age. Maybe smarter book-wise than he was now. He was beginning to think he was too old to be beginning a college career.

He shook off the cloud of uncertainty that was fogging his brain. "Will we be seeing you and Jack for dinner on Sunday?"

"Me, yes. I don't know about Jack."

"Is he on call?"

"Maybe."

Something was off with Autumn and Jack, but Neal wasn't going to push. He wouldn't want her pressing him about Anne.

"See you Sunday."

Autumn waved her fingers at him and breezed off to join a group of students congregating outside the classroom down the hall where his English class was held.

His less-than-stellar start lodged front and center

in his mind. Once he dropped off the solar assessment readings to Anne, he'd better stop by Professor Murray's office and see if she was in today.

He strode the few steps to the side corridor where Anne had her office. The door was half-open. He paused and studied her profile—the line of her patrician nose, wide mouth, determined chin— charmed that he could still see traces of the geeky teenager he'd befriended in high school. She nibbled a pretzel stick and clicked the computer mouse.

Neal tapped on the door and she spun around in the chair.

"Hi. I was reading an email from Gary. He's jazzed about going solar with the birthing center project."

He resisted the smile that tugged at his lips. If Anne's students could hear her with her professional defenses down, they wouldn't see her as such a stick.

She waved the pretzel at him. "Come in, sit down." She placed the pretzel on a napkin on her desk. "I was finishing my lunch."

Her desk phone rang as he eased into the chair across the desk from her.

"Excuse me." She picked up the receiver. "Dr. Howard. Three-thirty? I should be free. Let me check Outlook." Anne cradled the phone against her shoulder and checked her calendar on the computer. "Yes, that's fine."

She hung up the phone and returned her attention to Neal. "You completed the readings?" Her voice had lost its earlier excitement and taken on a more impersonal tone.

"Right here." He flipped open the cover of his clipboard. "Along with some diagrams I drew." He pulled several sheets from the clip and passed them across the table.

She leafed through the report he'd filled out. "Excellent. These are good." She tapped her finger on one of his designs. "You've done some drafting?"

"I have a CAD program I play around with," he said, glad he'd decided to toss the designs in.

She stacked the sheets in a neat pile. "I'll get these right out to Gary and have him send you his more developed designs directly."

Anne's innocuous words deflated Neal's pumped-up ego. He'd thought his designs were good, that she thought they were, too. But what did he expect? Gary was an engineer. Of course he'd spec out the designs.

"What we want you to do next is scope out some solar contractors."

Neal leaned forward in his seat. "Okay."

She picked up a folder on her desk and handed it to him. "Here's a list of vendors we've used on other projects and our general requirements. Gary… we thought you might have some local contacts."

His pulse ticked up. He didn't know anyone personally, but if there were any companies from here to Albany, he'd find them. "When would you like my recommendations?"

"We have time. The middle of next month would be fine."

"No problem." He paused, weighing whether to tell her about his interest in being a part of the solar collector installation. Some solar companies had their own electricians and others used subcontractors. The phone interrupted his musing.

"Excuse me, again." Anne's lips curved in a broad smile. "Margaret." Her voice rose in question and her face blanched.

She clutched the phone as if it were a lifeline. "No!"

With her free hand, Anne swiped at the tears that began streaming down her face. Neal rose and walked around the desk touching her shoulder as she slumped in her chair.

His touch reminded her that she wasn't alone. She steeled her muscles and regained her equilibrium, but let him keep his hand on her shoulder.

She cleared her throat. "Yes. No. I'll drive. Tomorrow at one. It's okay. I have GPS. I'm so sorry." Anne removed the phone from her ear and stared at the wall.

"Reenie." She sobbed and laid her head on arms on the desk.

Neal rubbed her back. She should sit up and pull herself together. She had that meeting at three-thirty. But she couldn't stop the tears, and Neal's touch was so comforting.

"Anne." His voice was soft and close, his breath brushing her ear.

She lifted her head and turned toward the sound. He squatted next to her chair.

"Sorry." She sniffed and, avoiding eye contact, opened a desk drawer and pulled out a tissue.

"What happened?"

She shook her head. She'd finally stopped the tears. Telling him would only start them again.

"What can I do?"

The edge to his voice drew her back to him. Maybe sharing would help. She breathed in and out twice. "My friend Reenie and her husband were in a car accident." She spoke quickly to get the words out before the tears began again. "They... they didn't make it."

"I'm so sorry."

She shuddered, but her eyes stayed dry. He wrapped his arm around her shoulders and eased her from the chair. She let him guide her to the small couch on the other side of her office and sit beside her.

"Margaret, Reenie's mother, didn't have my cell phone number or new house number." Her voice sounded far away, disembodied. "Margaret couldn't remember the name of the college. My mother is on a cruise with her new husband. She couldn't reach her, either. The funeral was Monday. I missed it."

"That's rough, really rough."

"I have to meet with their attorney tomorrow afternoon, in Sudbury."

Neal squeezed her shoulder. "That's near Boston."

She closed her eyes, wanting to blank it all out, and nodded.

"Do you have someone to go with you?"

Anne ran through the friends she'd made in Paradox and at the college. Jamie was the only one she felt close enough to to ask. And she wouldn't. It would put Jamie out too much. She'd have to arrange for someone to watch her kids. *Ian.* Reenie and Rob's baby. Had he been in the accident, too? Margaret hadn't said anything about him. Anne's chest tightened.

She cleared her throat. "I'll be fine. Sudbury is only about four hours away."

"I could go with you."

Warmth waved over her. But Neal coming with her wasn't a good idea. She'd broken down in front of him during the thunderstorm, let him see her vulnerable again today. Her late husband, Michael, had drilled her that the only way to succeed in a man's world was never to let people see her vulnerabilities. And, as far as she could tell, he'd been

right. She'd come so far from the nondescript book-
worm she'd been in high school and college.

"I won't take no for an answer."

She bristled. Now Neal sounded like Michael.
Would he hold her breakdown today and during the
storm against her? And there was no telling how
well she'd be able to hold things together once she
got to Sudbury. Neal rubbed her upper arm, and
she relaxed. He wasn't Michael. He wasn't anything like Michael.

She relented. "All right."

Neal removed his arm from her shoulder and
took her hands. "Would you like to pray?"

Anne jerked her head up and met his strong, clear
gaze. "Yes. Yes, I would." She closed her eyes and
bowed her head and let Neal's words of prayer wash
over her, lightening her heavy heart.

After the prayer he released her hands. "I'll call
Pastor Joel and put you and Reenie's family on the
Community Church prayer list."

His church prayer list. That was so public. "I'm
not a member," she stammered.

"I'll say it's a friend of mine."

Friend. Yes, they *were* friends, like they'd been
in high school. Tears pricked her eyes.

He lifted her chin with his finger. "I won't do it.
I didn't mean to upset you."

"No, no you didn't. It's…it's just the sort of thing
Reenie would do, pray with me, put me on a prayer

list." Things a true friend would do. "Thanks. For everything."

"You're welcome."

She glanced down at her watch to break eye contact before her unshed tears became real tears. "My meeting. I've got to get going."

"I'm sure they'll understand your missing it."

"No, I have responsibilities."

Responsibilities that were more important than grieving for her friend? Women were so hard to figure, and Anne even more so. She so often thought like a man. It threw him when she didn't. And today she seemed to be seesawing back and forth. She seemed devastated by her friend's death. But she was still all business.

Anne rose and moved to the desk. "I'll have to make arrangements for someone to cover my classes tomorrow or cancel them."

He hadn't given a thought to his classes. But it was only one day. How much could he miss? He pushed off the couch and crossed the room to her.

She picked up the solar report and put it back on the desk. "And get these out to Gary. I can do that after the meeting." She seemed to be talking more to herself than to him.

"You'll be okay tonight?"

Her eyes widened as if she'd just noticed he was still there. "Fine."

"I could stop by."

She fluttered her hands above the report. "You don't have to. I have a class at six, and papers I can grade when I get home."

Either Anne required her students to write a lot of papers or that was her signal for him to get lost. The sheen in her eyes as she looked up at him cut to the quick. This had nothing to do with him. She was coping the only way she seemed to know how, by making herself busy. He ran his hand over his cropped hair. If only he knew some way to make things easier for her.

"I'll pick you up about eight-thirty tomorrow morning."

"I'll be ready. Should I bring anything?" He was stalling. She might think she was fine, but her stop-and-start motions said otherwise.

"Maybe an overnight bag." She rubbed the bridge of her nose and curved her hair behind one ear. "Margaret wasn't entirely clear what the meeting was about. It all must have been so awful for her, alone in that big house. She's not well. If the meeting lasts long, we…I may not want to drive back tomorrow night. She may need me to stay." Anne's voice cracked. "I'm asking too much of you. You don't need to come."

He wasn't about to let her push him away again. "Like I said, I'll be ready at eight-thirty."

"Thanks." She breathed out. "For being a friend."

"No problem." He leaned against the desk and righted himself when it moved, or he thought it moved. He glanced at Anne. Her expression was inscrutable. "I'd better get going."

"I'll see you tomorrow morning. Thanks again."

"You're sure you'll be okay tonight?"

She frowned.

He'd done it again. Pushed when he should have backed off.

"I'll be fine. Jamie's right next door if I need someone."

"Good."

Neal left Anne's office before he could come up with another reason to stay. Jamie was a good friend. She'd take care of Anne—if Anne called her. He reheard the crack in Anne's voice as she told him she was asking too much of him. Didn't the woman know it was okay to let friends help? He kicked a wad of paper across the hall floor, looked around and crossed over to pick it up. He crumpled it in his fist.

Anne had said they were friends. He popped into an open classroom and tossed the paper in a wastebasket at the front of the room. Score one for Hazard. He slipped out of the classroom. Friends was good. More than friends might be better. Neal stopped short. For the first time in a long time, he just might be ready to try a relationship with a woman that went beyond simple friendship.

Chapter Nine

Anne wiped the smeared mascara from beneath her eyes and applied under-eye concealer. It did little to cover the evidence of her sleepless night. What did it matter anyway? Except she didn't want Neal to know she'd alternately cried herself to sleep and kept herself awake. She finished her makeup and decided it was as good as it was going to get. The weather was supposed to be sunny. She could hide behind her sunglasses. She grabbed them from her dresser and her overnight bag from the bed and loaded it into her car. Ten minutes later, she was at the turn to the Hazards' campground.

Her heartbeat quickened exponentially the closer she got to their log home. Four hours alone in the car with Neal. She could do it, hold herself together without exposing any more personal information. They could talk about the birthing center project, solar energy, Neal's classes, Neal's business, his daughter, Autumn. She ticked off safe subjects.

She stepped from the car and took in the cloudless blue sky over the towering pines that obscured Paradox Lake. The tranquility left her breathless and calmed her still racing heart.

Lord, with Your help, I can make it through today. Her words were as much an affirmation as a prayer. But she didn't think He would mind.

She marched up the shale walk to the front door and knocked.

Mary answered the door with a broad smile. "Annie. Come in. I couldn't imagine who would be at our front door so early in the morning."

Anne lost some of her bravado. Neal hadn't told his parents about coming with her? Or had he changed his mind? It wasn't like she couldn't make the drive alone. But despite her qualms, she was looking forward to Neal's company.

"Everyone uses the side door through the garage. But you wouldn't know that." Mary waved her through the living room. "Neal's in the kitchen. I'm so sorry to hear about your friend."

"Thank you." Anne didn't need to say more, even though Mary's open expression invited her to.

Neal met them at the doorway between the kitchen and living room. "Hi."

"Hi." Filling the doorway, he looked dark and attractive, radiating strength and security. The opposite of how she was feeling and, though she hated to admit it, just what she needed today.

"Do you have time for a cup of coffee?" Mary asked.

Anne remembered the homey atmosphere of the barbeque at Emily and Drew's and imagined breakfast at the Hazards' would be equally warm. A family warmth that she'd found equally inviting and excluding. "No, thank you. We should be going."

She turned to Neal. "Are you ready?"

"Yes." He lifted his athletic bag.

"You can go out the front door," Mary said.

"Just like company. Thanks, Mom."

She gave him a playful swat.

"As kids, Mom always kept the front door locked. We had to use the kitchen door so that we didn't track dirt across the rug."

"Yeah, Neal's middle name could have been dirt."

"Emily said that you liked working outside, helping your dad with the campground."

"During the summer, he would have lived outside if we'd let him."

"Ah, Mom, we need to be leaving. You can tell Anne all about my childhood some other time."

Was that a tinge of pink on Neal's cheeks? Anne hid a smile. She'd like to hear more about Neal as a youngster. Michael had been so much older, making Anne's mother-in-law more her grandmother's age. They'd never developed a rapport. While she could easily imagine Neal as a boy, she had no idea what Michael might have been like.

Anne shook the thoughts from her head.

"I'm sorry, Anne. I sometimes get carried away talking about Neal, Emily and Autumn."

Where had Mary gotten the idea she wasn't interested? She was too interested. "Pardon?"

"You shook your head," Neal said.

"I…I was thinking about something else. But we do need to get on the road."

"Drive carefully," Mary said.

Neal opened the front door and let Anne precede him.

When they reached her car, Anne handed him the keys, remembering him telling her he wasn't a good passenger. "Why don't you drive the first part of the trip, and I'll drive when we get close to Boston where I'm familiar with the area streets?"

"Sounds good. I don't mind admitting that I'm not a fan of city driving."

So Neal had his weak spots, too. And didn't seem to have any qualms about admitting them. Some of the gray cloud that had been hanging over Anne since yesterday lifted.

Rather than taking the interstate south to Albany and catching the thruway east to the Massachusetts Turnpike as she would have done, Neal started out on Route 74 toward Vermont.

"Wouldn't the interstate be quicker?" Anne asked.

"No, this way is more direct and has no traffic to contend with. It should cut some time off the trip."

Anne was too thankful for the company to argue. And the picturesque scenery was calming. Here and there, the trees still clung on to a few vibrant red-and-orange leaves.

"This must have been gorgeous a couple of weeks ago. The trees," she added when Neal didn't immediately respond.

"I guess. A lot of people drive up north in the fall to see the foliage. I'm afraid I take it for granted."

"It's easy to do, not appreciate what we have." Michael had been like that. Her, too, always reaching for something more.

Neal's mouth twisted down.

"Like I never noticed the trees turning on the drive from home to the college, although I'm sure they have." She filled in the brief moment of silence and waited.

"Sorry," Neal said after a few moments. "I was thinking about something else."

"I appreciate your coming with me today. I hope it doesn't mess up your schedule too much. I know you have work and classes."

"I can handle it."

Obviously, she'd taken the conversation in the wrong direction. But she couldn't figure out where she'd gotten off course.

"I don't mind." His voice softened. "I didn't

have anything going on that couldn't wait. Why don't you tell me about your friend Reenie…if you want?"

Surprisingly, Anne found that she did. "We were college roommates," she started, and the miles flew by as she regaled him with their college escapades and how they'd reconnected when Reenie and her husband had moved back to the Boston area shortly after Michael's death.

They passed through a corner of New Hampshire and into Massachusetts. "Want me to take over the driving now? You've driven most of the way."

"Actually, I'm okay, if you want to give me directions once we get close."

"We're close now. Margaret's home is in the Carding Mill section of the Wayside Inn historic district." She laughed. "But that doesn't mean anything to you."

"Got me there."

Anne rattled off a series of directions that brought them to the drive leading to Reenie's mother's home. It wound through at least an acre of lushly landscaped and treed lawn before ending at a large traditional single-style New England home overlooking a large pond.

Neal whistled. "I'll bet you could fit the whole camp lodge in half of that house."

Anne had gone home with Reenie numerous times during their college years, but she didn't remember the house being so large or ostentatious. It had simply been Reenie's home.

Neal was out of the car and around to her side to open the door before she'd even reached for the door handle. They walked the white stone path to the front door and rang the doorbell. It chimed their arrival.

The door swung open to reveal an impeccably dressed and coiffed woman in a wheelchair.

"Anne. I'm so glad you're here."

She bent down into the older woman's arms and hugged her. "Me, too."

The woman released her. "Please come in." She turned her wheelchair and led them into an entryway with a cathedral ceiling and walnut staircase that rivaled his parents' living room in size.

"Margaret," Anne said when the woman stopped by the doorway to another room and turned back toward them. "This is my friend Neal Hazard. Neal, Margaret Cabot."

Neal took Margaret's extended hand. "Nice to meet you. I'm so sorry for your loss."

Margaret's eyes clouded and her lip quivered. "Thank you." She released his hand. "Is your luggage in the car?" She looked from Neal to Anne.

"Gammy! Where you?" A red-headed boy who looked to Neal to be no more than two and a half or three, at the most, raced through the doorway and came to an abrupt stop in front of Anne.

"Nee Nee," he said and looked around her. "Mommy?"

The plaintive question socked Neal in the gut. The little guy must be Anne's godson. He hadn't connected Reenie with the child Anne had talked about at the barbeque.

Anne stood statue-still.

"Ian." Margaret leaned forward in her chair, arms out. "Remember, Mommy and Daddy are in heaven with the angels."

"No!" He stomped his foot and his face crumpled.

A teen with short spiky hair rushed in. "Mrs. Cabot. I'm so sorry. I tripped over Ian's blocks and he got away from me."

Margaret smiled at the girl. "Jessica has been helping me with Ian. Her grandmother is my next-door neighbor. Jessica, this is Anne and…"

A howl from Ian drowned out the rest of the introduction. Jessica scooped him up.

"No," he shouted and kicked. "Nee Nee, Mommy."

Anne flinched and took Ian from the girl. "It's okay, sweetie. Aunt Annie has you." She rubbed his back and he sobbed against her shoulder.

The cries tore at Neal's heart. "Poor little guy," he said as much to himself as to anyone else.

Ian lifted his head and looked at Neal over Anne's shoulder. "Who dat?" He sniffled and pointed.

"That's Aunt Annie's friend Neal," his grandmother said.

Ian looked from Anne to Neal and, then, at Margaret. "Nal."

"Close enough," Neal said.

While Ian didn't quite smile, his cheeks dimpled. He hid his face in Anne's shoulder again and slowly peered over it at Neal again.

"Boo!" Neal said.

Ian responded with a sniffle that turned into a giggle. He scrunched his eyes closed and popped them open. "Boo!" He mimicked Neal.

Neal's heart swelled.

"I hate to interrupt," Margaret said. "Especially since Ian is usually so shy with people he doesn't know."

A corner of Neal's mouth quirked up in a crooked smile. "What can I say? I'm a kid magnet. I inherited it from my dad."

Margaret gave him a look of warm approval. "But Anne and I have to leave for our meeting. Jessica, you'll be okay with Ian?"

"We'll be fine. I'll read to him and see if I can get him down for a nap. I brought some homework I can do while he sleeps."

Ian wimpered.

"If he sleeps."

"Neal, there's a gym downstairs. Rob keeps..." Margaret's voice caught. "Kept extra workout clothes in the foot locker. Or there's a library in the turret. Anne can show you the way and meet me outside."

"Thanks." A gym and a library. More than a little out of his element.

He watched Anne hand Ian to Jessica and noticed the quality of Anne's clothes compared to the teen's casual jeans and T-shirt. Not that he knew anything about women's fashion but the perfect fit of Anne's simple dark blue dress said tailored for her. Light from the tall windows glinted off the bracelet watch dangling from her wrist. He swallowed. This was Anne's element. They were from different worlds. That should be enough to quell his growing attraction. But it wasn't. Not by a long shot.

"No!" Ian struggled out of Jessica's arms and dropped to the floor.

Anne squatted to his level. She and Margaret were due at the lawyer's office in twenty minutes. "I have to go out with Grandma for a while. Jessica is going to read you stories."

He shook his head. "Nal." He pointed to Neal.

"You want Neal to read you a story?"

Ian nodded.

Anne exchanged a glance with Margaret.

"It's your decision." Margaret looked down at her lap and turned the ring on her finger.

What did the older woman mean it was her decision? She searched her face, but Margaret kept her eyes lowered.

Neal broke the undercurrent in the room. "I don't mind watching him."

Ian looked up at the sound of his deep voice and stuck his finger in his mouth, his eyes shiny with unshed tears.

"We shouldn't be too long." She looked to Margaret for confirmation. The woman was totally focused on her grandson. Anne couldn't shake the feeling she'd done something to hurt her. But she hadn't.

"We'll be fine, won't we, bud?" He crouched next to Anne, close enough for her to smell the outdoorsy scent of his soap or, could be, aftershave.

"Rob, his dad, called him that—bud." Margaret's voice was thin, barely above a whisper.

Ian sucked his finger as if his life depended on it. Helplessness washed over Anne. She reached for the toddler, but he brushed by her and flung himself at Neal.

"Whoa." Neal fought for his balance and lost, tumbling onto his back.

Ian scrambled up his sprawled form and kneeled on his chest. "Nal?"

The quiver in the child's voice shot through Anne like a jolt of electricity.

He touched Neal's face.

"Grrrr." Neal rolled to a sitting position and hugged the little guy tight.

Ian laughed. "More."

Anne rose and released her pent-up breath. She turned to Margaret. "This may be a good time for us to slip out."

"Do you think that's a good idea?"

The older woman's question struck her more as a reprimand. Why was Margaret acting like she needed Anne's permission concerning Ian? Compassion pushed away her slight irritation. Margaret must be overwhelmed by everything that had happened and being responsible for an active little boy.

"They'll be fine." She pointed at the two guys play-wrestling on the floor. "Neal's a single parent. He has lots of experience."

"I'm sure you're right. I've never seen Ian take to anyone like he has to Neal." Margaret pursed her lips. "What I meant was whether leaving Ian without saying goodbye, making sure he understands that we'll be back, was a good idea."

"Of course." Anne hadn't thought of that at all. Another squeal from Ian drew her to the two of them romping. Neal would have.

"Hey, guys."

Neal righted himself and stood, Ian in his arms.

He looked so in control with a beaming Ian resting his head against Neal's.

She touched the toddler's chubby cheek. "Grammy and I have to go now. Neal's going to stay with you."

"Yes, Nal!"

Margaret rolled her chair closer. "Grammy and Aunt Annie will bring you home some popcorn chicken." She raised her hand to shield her mouth. "It's his favorite and I've indulged him too often lately, but…" She shrugged her shoulders.

This was more like the doting grandma she knew Margaret to be.

"Chick'n for Nal, too?"

"Of course, for Neal, too."

"And what do you think?" Neal nodded toward Anne. "Should we let Aunt Annie have some?"

"'Course." Ian parroted his grandmother.

Margaret reached up to Ian and Neal leaned so that she could give him a kiss. "Be a good boy for Neal."

"Ian good boy." He pointed at himself.

"Oh, yes, you are." His grandmother rubbed noses with him. She cleared her throat. "Jessica, Anne and I can drop you home on our way to the lawyer's. I'll pay you for the whole day."

"You don't have to do that, Mrs. Cabot."

"Yes, I do. I don't know what I would have done without you."

The teen shuffled her feet. "You know I love this guy." She ruffled Ian's red curls. "I'll miss you."

"Miss you," he piped.

Margaret and Jessica's words weighed heavy on Anne. Must be the teen was on some kind of school break.

"Bye, bye, Ian. Aunt Annie will see you later."

Ian's "later" made them all laugh.

"I'll get my backpack and meet you out in the garage," Jessica said.

"Okay. Show Neal where Ian's room is first and meet us in the garage." Margaret spun her chair toward the hall to the side of the entryway.

That sounded more like the Margaret Anne knew. She gave Ian and Neal another wave goodbye, struck again by how natural he and Ian looked together, and followed Margaret out through the dining room and kitchen.

"Reenie talked to you about their wills, didn't she?"

Anne thought for a moment. Reenie had said she and Rob were having wills made and that they wanted to make sure Ian would be raised in a Christian home. Rob's parents couldn't provide that. Margaret could. Anne watched the older woman maneuver the ramp from the kitchen door to the garage. She must be having unnecessary—in Anne's opinion—doubts about being responsible for Ian. Margaret and her husband had done a great job with Reenie. To Anne, Margaret had always seemed a natural mother. And she had the resources to hire a nanny and any other help she needed with Ian.

"Yes, she did." Her mind raced through the conversation she remembered having with Reenie and used the lack of any more details to quell the uneasiness her reassurance invoked. But she'd been preoccupied with the arrangements for transitioning the responsibility for Green Spaces' operation so she could take the position at NCCC. Was there something she'd missed? Her throat constricted. Reenie had always been there to listen to her.

"Good." Margaret nodded. "I wanted to make sure there weren't any surprises at the attorney's office."

Chapter Ten

Neal heard the hum of Margaret's chair rolling down the hardwood floor of the hall outside Ian's room. He rose from the rocking chair, placed the youngster in the toddler bed and raised the side rail. When he turned from the bed, Margaret was in the doorway.

"How was he?"

"I think I can recite *Where the Wild Things Are* by heart. Every time I'd think he was asleep and go to put him in bed, he'd open his eyes and say 'again.'"

Margaret's eyes were soft and a half smile curved her lips. "He does love that story. His daddy got it for him. It was Rob's favorite story when he was small." She backed out of the doorway. "Turn the intercom on and let's go downstairs."

She led him to what looked like sliding oak doors. Margaret flicked a switch on the wall and the doors glided open to reveal an elevator. He stepped in with her.

"My husband had it installed soon after my multiple sclerosis was diagnosed. I was so angry with him. He'd jumped the gun, but I was thankful for his thoughtfulness when I had to start using the chair. He was gone by then." She waved her hand. "I'm rambling. And I don't have Reenie to stop me."

Neal inched away from the wheelchair. Was she going to lose it? Where was Anne?

The elevator stopped and the doors opened. He released his pent-up breath.

Margaret rolled forward into another hall. "Sorry about that."

Guilt pricked Neal. Margaret had been through a lot. What was a little rambling? "No problem. Where's Anne?"

"Walking by the pond."

His heart constricted. "I take it the reading was rough on her."

Margaret twisted her ring. "Her reaction. I didn't expect it." The older woman's voice rose in what sounded to Neal like anger.

He tensed. She was obviously overwrought. But he couldn't imagine what Anne could have said to upset her so much.

"Go talk with her." Margaret leaned forward. "Please. Anne needs you."

Margaret's words ignited a protective feeling in him he preferred not to analyze.

"You'll be all right? With Ian upstairs?"

"I'll get my book from the living room." She pointed down the hall. "And go up and try to read in my room. Go." The last word was a plea.

Neal let himself out the way he and Anne had come in, glad for the cool brisk breeze that rustled the few leaves that hadn't been removed from the manicured lawn. He hadn't realized how warm the house had been. He came around the back side of the house. Anne's dark blue dress stood out among the greens, browns and muted yellows of the lawn and the fading fall foliage by the pond. He paused and watched her for a moment. What did Margaret expect him to do, to say? He raised his face to the afternoon sun and closed his eyes.

"Lord, please guide me. Lend me Your wisdom to help Margaret and Anne. In Your goodness, relieve them of their pain as only You can."

The sun moved behind a cloud, sending a chill through him. Not the answer he was looking for.

"I ask this in Your name. Amen." He raised his head and hiked down to the pond.

Anne stood statute-still, staring out over the water. If she heard him approach, she gave no sign.

"Anne." He broke the silence, his voice too loud, too rough to his ears.

"Margaret told you?"

He stepped closer. "She just said you were out here and might need someone to talk to."

"Reenie and Rob named me as Ian's guardian." She breathed deeply as if needing fuel for her next word. "I didn't know."

From the look on her face, Anne felt as sucker-punched as he had when Autumn's mother had told him she was pregnant.

"What am I going to do?" Her soft words hung between them.

He put his arm around her shoulder. "You're going to be the best mother to Ian you can be."

She shuddered and turned into his arms. "I can't. I just can't. I'm not ready. I don't know how to be a parent."

"No one is ever really ready."

"Everything Ian is used to is here. His grandmother. His day care. Everything."

He rubbed her back and held her to him. Her vulnerability touched his heart. "You'll be fine. Ian will be fine." *In time,* he added to himself.

"But I didn't know." She sobbed. "Reenie must have told me. Margaret thought I knew. I wasn't a good enough friend to listen and hear something as important as that." Her voice took on a bitter edge. "I was too wrapped up in myself. My new job. My new life."

She pushed at him, but he continued to hold her, wanting to protect her from her grief and self-condemnation.

"You don't understand. Can't understand." She spoke into his chest, muffling her words.

"Then tell me."

"I'm not the person Reenie thought I was. I can't be the mother Ian needs. Do you know why she and Rob chose me?" She raised her head, challenge radiating from her tear-filled eyes. "They wanted Ian to be raised in a good Christian home. Ha! I can't even decide which church to attend."

"Being a good Christian doesn't hinge on which church you go to. Reenie could see into your heart. She knew you would treasure Ian just as she and Rob did. Teach him about our Lord as Reenie taught you."

She dropped her head as if it were too much effort to keep her face lifted to him. "I'll let them down."

"God doesn't give us more than we can handle." He raised her chin with his finger and she grimaced.

How many people had told him that when Autumn was small? And he hadn't believed them any more than Anne believed him.

"How can it be God's will to rip Ian from everything he knows? I've gone over and over it in my head. I have to be missing something. Wasn't it enough to take his parents from him? Or am I supposed to leave the college and come back here? I don't think I can do it. Is that selfish? Does that make me a bad person?" Anne's voice rose with each word.

Her anguish was too much for him. He did the only thing he could think of to comfort her. The thing he'd wanted to do since the thunderstorm. He leaned toward her and brushed her lips with his. She stiffened, then gave in, tilting her head back and placing her hands on his shoulders. He accepted the silent invitation, increasing the pressure and encircling her waist with his arms.

Soft. Sweet. It would be so easy to lose himself in the pleasure of having her near. The loud honking of a flock of geese overhead stopped him.

Neal stepped back, and she blinked at him as if trying to bring him into focus. He cleared his throat. "You're not alone. You have friends to help you. Jamie, Emily, me."

"You'd all do that?"

"Of course."

Uneasiness followed his quick affirmation. He shouldn't speak for the others, make promises he couldn't keep. But he could help her with Ian without getting involved. Their kiss notwithstanding. It could be fun watching the little guy grow knowing he wasn't his responsibility.

The sun moved out from behind the clouds, its

bright rays emphasizing the tears drying on Anne's cheeks. He resisted an urge wipe the last of them away with his thumb.

Her lips quivered. "You're right. I have to think of Ian, honor Reenie and Rob's wishes."

Neal would have liked to see her a little more fired up. Reenie had entrusted Anne with her most important treasure. At least he thought of Autumn that way. Raising her hadn't been easy. She'd certainly put him through the gauntlet and tried his patience in ways he couldn't have ever imagined it could be tried. But there wasn't a time since her birth that he didn't want her with his whole heart.

Neal looked at Anne, so small and slight in the shadows of the towering willows surrounding the pond. His thoughts were unfair. In his heart, he couldn't believe that Anne didn't want Ian every bit as much.

She crossed her arms and squeezed herself as though she were cold. He returned his arm to her shoulder. "We should get back up to the house."

Anne nodded and let him direct her away from the pond.

"I should call Mom. I mean, she'll worry. I said we'd probably be back this evening." He pressed his lips together before any more words blubbered out. "And I need to call a local car rental place for a car to drive back to Paradox tomorrow."

"Maybe you should hold off calling about the car until tomorrow."

His heart leaped. She wanted him to stay and drive back with her and Ian. He did a mental rundown of his work and school schedules for the rest of the week. Nothing he couldn't rearrange workwise.

"I can stay a few days, if you want me to." She did want him to stay, didn't she?

Her eyes clouded in question. "Oh, I don't think that'll be necessary."

His shoulders slumped. He'd really misread that one.

"We should be able to leave tomorrow."

Neal gazed down at Anne. An infantry division would be easier to move that fast than a three-year-old. "You can have Ian ready to go that quickly?"

He regretted his question as soon as it was out. She shot him a shattered look before she whirled and ran into the house.

Anne closed the door against the world and retreated into the room Margaret had given her for the night. She was sure she'd been like a zombie at dinner. But Margaret and Neal didn't understand. They couldn't understand. She didn't know how to be a parent. Her parents were no example, and she hadn't spent enough time with her grandmother, who was.

Michael had repeatedly told her she was more cut out for academics or business than for motherhood. Hadn't her few disastrous outings with Michael's children proven that?

Rubbing the bridge of her nose, she hoped the dull ache in her neck wasn't a forewarning of a migraine. She hadn't had one since she'd moved to Paradox and hadn't brought her prescription with her. A baby picture of Ian on the wall made her swallow hard. Sure, she wanted children. But she'd assumed she'd have a helpmate who knew what he was doing. She lifted her overnight bag to the bed and took out her things.

Someone like Neal. She tried to shake that thought from her head. But her traitorous mind flashed to the kiss they'd shared by the pond. Rationally, she knew it was nothing except him trying to console her in the way that came easiest to men. But her heart had latched onto the possibility that it was a promise of more. Once again, she'd let her guard down, as it was so easy to do with Neal. Somehow, he made her feel safe sharing her inner self, even though she knew the consequences of letting anyone see a crack in her armor.

Neal was a friend, like Jamie, nothing more. That's all he'd ever be. For so many reasons. And especially now that she had Ian. Emily had said Neal was adamant about not having any more children. She snapped the bag and her heart shut.

But her doubts still plagued her. What were Reenie and Rob thinking, choosing her as Ian's guardian? Not only was she not parent material, she wasn't even sure she knew how to be a good Christian. If she were, wouldn't she be able to talk with God and receive answers? All she got was more questions.

She put her case at the end of the bed, crawled under the covers and squeezed her eyes shut. Neal was right, she needed to ignore the doubts and questions and put herself in God's hands.

"Lord." Anne spoke aloud into the darkness. "Help me trust Your timing and be obedient to Your calling for my life."

She stopped and lay perfectly still waiting for something. Anything. When nothing came, her mind replayed the past two days over and over like a fast-forward of a bad movie. Everything the lawyer had said. Everything Margaret had said in words and implication. Everything Neal had said. The words tumbled around her head until she shut them out and made herself think analytically.

She weighed moving back to the Boston area against bringing Ian to Paradox Lake. The house wasn't baby-proof, as if she knew what baby-proofed was. She tried to picture Ian playing on the floor of her office at the college, at the day care center where Jamie took Opal. Nothing felt right. What wasn't she factoring in? If Reenie were here, she'd say Anne was trying too hard, like she did with everything. But Reenie wasn't here. She'd never be able to call on her for guidance again.

Chapter Eleven

The honking of more migrating geese on the pond woke her from the sleep that had finally come in the early hours of the morning. Sleep that had come only after she'd made a decision. Lulled by the dimly lit room, Anne assumed it was still early until she looked at the alarm clock. Ten o'clock. She hadn't slept this late since college. She rolled out of bed and pulled the curtain aside. A gray dismal New England morning greeted her. She shook off the gloom, dressed and went downstairs. The low rumble of Neal's voice and the smell of coffee drew her to the kitchen.

"Good morning, sleepy-head." Neal turned from the sink where Ian stood on a step stool beside him.

The rightness of the picture they made sent a ripple of apprehension through her.

"Seepy-head." Ian echoed. "I washing dishes." He lifted a blue plastic cup covered in bubbles.

"So I see. Do you have a coffee cup for me?"

Ian poured the water from the cup into the sink. "Nope."

"Here you go." Neal handed her a mug and spoon from the dishwasher.

"Thanks." She made a cup of coffee in Margaret's gourmet single-cup coffee brewer, carried it across the room and added exactly a half teaspoon of sugar from the bowl on the table. "Where's Margaret?"

Neal guided Ian's hand and another cupful of water back over the sink. "Doctor's appointment."

"She should have said something yesterday. I would have driven her."

"Maria, her housekeeper, drove her."

"Good. I know Maria. She's been with Margaret a long time, since Reenie and I were in college."

"Ria and Ian make cookies." The toddler climbed down and pushed the stool toward the other end of the counter.

"Whoa, buddy. What's up?"

"Cookies." He pointed at a ceramic Pooh Bear. "For Nee Nee."

Anne checked Neal's expression before she nodded. Her first inclination had been to say no. As a child, she'd only gotten treats when her parents judged she'd earned them. Neal's indulgent half smile changed her mind and bolstered her confidence that she'd made the right decision.

"Okay. I'll get some cookies for Aunt Annie and you."

"Nal, too."

"Me, too." Neal lifted Pooh's head and pulled out three cookies. "In your seat, buddy." He handed the cookies to Anne on a napkin and put Ian in his booster seat. Anne and Neal sat beside him.

Anne handed a cookie to Ian and Neal.

"Thanks."

"Tanks." Ian bit into the treat and grinned his mother's grin, crumbs falling to the table in front of him.

Anne dropped her gaze and took a big swig of her coffee to quell the sadness and longing inside her.

"Hello." A bright voice pulled her from her self-absorbed gloom.

Margaret's neighbor's daughter, Jessica, breezed into the kitchen. "Is Ian all ready for story hour?"

Neal used the napkin to wipe the cookie crumbs from Ian's face and hands, slipped his plastic smock off and rolled down his shirtsleeves. "All set." He lifted the toddler to the floor.

Jessica took Ian's hand.

"Wait." Anne's strident tone stopped the duo in their tracks. "Who's driving?"

The teen's forehead wrinkled. "Mom. Why?"

Neal gave Anne an understanding smile.

"Nothing. Never mind. You guys have a good time."

Jessica stepped forward, but Ian stayed rooted where he was.

"Come on Nee Nee and Nal." He waved his hand toward the door.

Anne went over and kneeled next to Ian. "Aunt Annie and Neal can't come today. You go ahead with Jessica. We'll be here when you get back."

Ian cocked his head to the side and looked from Anne to Neal. "Gammy, too?"

"Yes, Grandma will be here when you get back," Neal assured him. "Remember, she said she'd come right home from her doctor's appointment."

The little guy's fear wrapped itself around Anne's heart and squeezed. A sign that she'd made the right decision?

"We're going to play with Play-Doh today," Jessica coaxed.

"Play-Doh?" Bright-eyed, he looked from Jessica to Anne and Neal for confirmation.

"Play-Doh's cool stuff," Neal said.

"Okay."

"Give me a hug." Anne opened her arms. Ian threw himself at her, planted a sloppy kiss on her cheek and pulled away before she was ready to let him go.

"Bye, bye." He waved and pulled Jessica toward the door.

Anne and Neal waved back.

"Ditched for Play-Doh." She accepted the hand Neal offered to help her up.

"Pretty tough competition if you ask me."

Anne swallowed the lump in her throat and tried to match Neal's teasing tone. "But I hate coming in second. I like to win. Remember Science Olympiad?"

"Only too well." Neal laughed, but his laugh had a hollow ring to it that left her feeling she somehow didn't measure up. She shook it off. Neal wasn't judgmental like Michael had been.

"Did Margaret say when she'll be back?"

"In an hour or so."

"I'm going to warm up my coffee." She retrieved her cup and carried it to the coffee brewer. "Want to join me?"

"No, thanks." He leaned against the counter. "Before Margaret left, she said that Jessica and Maria had boxed Ian's clothes and toys and brought them here so you and she wouldn't have to go to Reenie and Rob's house."

The house that Reenie was restoring, that she was so proud of. Anne's hand shook as she lifted the cup from the coffee brewer. Margaret had done so much, seemed so in control despite her grief.

Now she could do something in return for Margaret and Ian.

She walked to the table.

"If you want, I can start loading Ian's things in the car. It'll give you more time with Margaret and to get Ian ready to go."

"You don't have to." She took a sip of the hot black liquid to fortify herself. "I was going to wait until Margaret got back and tell both of you together."

"What's up?"

"Last night when I went upstairs, I prayed like you said." She searched his face for approval. "At first, I didn't get any answer. Then, in the middle of the night I realized what I need to do."

Neal's lips thinned as if he suspected she was going to say something he wouldn't like. But it wasn't his decision. Wasn't for him to like or dislike.

She wiped her free hand against her jeans. "To do about Ian. And Margaret. Helping Ian adjust. To the changes, to everything." She was babbling. She didn't babble. She faced a classroom of college students every day, had lectured halls filled with engineers and scientists at conferences, and never stuttered a word. But for some reason, she couldn't get the words out to tell Neal her plan.

Anne placed the coffee mug on the table so Neal

wouldn't see her hand tremble. She should have waited for Margaret to return.

"I weighed all of the factors and the best solution I could come up with is to hire a nanny to help Margaret so Ian can stay here. I'm sure Margaret will agree."

"The best solution," Neal repeated. "This isn't some kind of mathematical equation. It's a little boy's life."

"Don't make me sound so cold. I'm not horrible. I thought about everything and everyone."

"No, I don't think you're horrible. I think you're overwhelmed and scared. And you did what's easiest for you. Let money take care of it."

Her anger surged. How could he even think that? "I tried your way, prayer, and as usual got nothing for my effort."

"Not my way. *His* way," Neal corrected her.

His superiority fueled her anger. "Well, I couldn't leave Margaret hanging. I had to do something."

He stared at her, stone-faced.

Her better judgment told her she should stop, but she couldn't stand him thinking her selfish and uncaring. "Sometimes you do have to think about yourself. Look at where you might be now if you'd done some thinking about your future back in high school. Left Autumn with your parents or her mother's parents and gone to RPI. Wouldn't that have been better in the long run?"

He blanched. "You don't know me at all if you think that's a choice I would make."

His response brooked no further argument. How had she let the conversation get so out of hand? She never let her anger get the best of her, was almost always open to opposing views, even when she was right.

Neal pushed away from the counter.

Anne let go of the mug handle and rested her hand on the table edge. "I'm sorry. I was presumptuous to think I know what would have been best for you."

"Yes. You were. I'm going to go see about a rental car." He strode from the room before she could get another word out.

Anne collapsed in the closest chair, the one Neal had been sitting in earlier. His residual warmth on the seat chilled her. Her decision about Ian had to be the right one. It had come to her after she'd prayed. Wasn't that the way it worked? And if she were following God's plan, things would work out with her and Neal and their friendship. What if they didn't? Did that mean they weren't meant to be friends for some good reason? She laid her head on her forearms on the table. She'd tried so hard. Why couldn't she hear His word?

Anne was a real piece of work. Neal threw his belongings in his athletic bag, and listened for the honk of the taxi he'd called to take him to the car rental place. Fortunately, the taxi service had said they could have a car here in fifteen minutes. Any more contact with Anne today and he'd totally lose his temper.

She'd been right yesterday at the pond when she'd said he couldn't understand. He couldn't. How could she turn her back on Ian? Sure, Margaret loved him. But obviously, she wasn't well, and she'd said she agreed with Reenie and Rob's choice of Anne. Anne's decision had Neal wondering how closely Reenie had stayed in contact with her since college. Anne had said Reenie and Rob had moved back to the Boston area not too long ago. Reenie might not have known Anne as she was now, the consummate businessperson, and based her choice on the younger, softer Anne she'd known in college, the girl he'd known in high school.

And where was Anne coming from, criticizing *his* life choices? He'd only been seventeen when Autumn was born, but he'd accepted his responsibilities. Anne was what, thirty-three, thirty-four, and her idea of accepting her responsibilities was to throw money at them? Neal ripped the zipper to the bag shut. He knew he was being unfair. She might have her reasons for her decision, good reasons, although he couldn't think what those reasons might be. And it wasn't like he hadn't thought of what his life might have been if he'd gone to college right out of high school.

The taxi's horn blasted outside. He took the stairs to the main floor two at a time, slowing his pace when he hit the last stair. He should tell Anne he was leaving. Leaving his bag by the front door, he went to the kitchen but she wasn't there. He didn't have time to go in search of her. Besides, the frame of mind he was in, it was probably best they didn't talk for a while.

Anne watched from the upstairs window as the taxi drove away, telling herself she *was* right. She was doing what was best for Ian now. It didn't mean she and Margaret couldn't change the arrangement later. Dropping the curtain, she surveyed the room. Might as well straighten up and make the bed to pass the time waiting for Margaret to return.

As she pulled the bedspread over the pillows, Anne heard a car approach the house. Her pulse quickened. Had Neal changed his mind? She hurried back to the window. *No.* It was Margaret and Maria. Anne finished making the bed and went downstairs.

"Hi," Margaret greeted her. "Did Ian go to his story hour at the library? He loves being with the other kids."

Margaret's words bolstered Anne's tenuous conviction that Ian should stay here with his familiar routines. "Yes, he did. He was a little reluctant, but Jessica told him they were going to use Play-Doh, and he all but dragged her from the house."

Margaret laughed. "He does like his Play-Doh. You should check and see if your local library has story hour for preschoolers. I think most of them do."

Anne had no idea if the Schroon Lake Public Library had preschool programs. She hadn't even been there since she'd moved to Paradox Lake. The college library had everything she needed. Not that it mattered if Ian was going to stay here with Margaret. Make that *since* he was going to stay.

Anne pushed her hair behind her ears. "We need to talk."

"Yes, we do. I've written down a few things for you about Ian."

Anne swallowed.

"The list is in the living room." Margaret led Anne down the hall to a well-appointed but homey room. "Here it is." She picked up a small notebook from a mission-style end table and flipped it open. "Sit, please." She motioned to the side chair across from her. "I'm getting a crick in my neck from looking up at you."

Anne perched on the edge of the chair. Margaret's smile told her she was kidding, but that didn't make broaching her plan for Ian any easier. "I've made an important decision. I think Ian should stay here with you."

Margaret's smile faded. "I can't take care of an active toddler." She patted the armrest of her wheelchair.

"Please hear me out." Anne reached over the space between them and put her hand over the older woman's. It was cool to her touch. "I'll hire a nanny, anything you need to help you."

Margaret pursed her lips.

"That didn't come out right." Anne shook her head. She didn't want Margaret to think she didn't want Ian like Neal had said. "Ian's life has been so disrupted. I don't want to disrupt it more. Everything that's familiar to him is here."

Margaret squeezed her hand. "I know. Don't you think I've thought of that, too? And about hiring a nanny?"

Anne's heart lightened. Neal's reaction had undermined her confidence in her decision.

"But a nanny isn't the same as a…" Margaret cleared her throat. "As a mother. I know. A nanny raised me. My parents divorced and my father had custody. A five-year-old didn't fit well in my mother's new life. I loved my nanny. She stayed with us as our housekeeper when I was older. But she wasn't a mother."

"*You'll* be here." Anne wished her words hadn't come out sounding so strident. Margaret *would* think she didn't want Ian, like Neal thought.

"For how long? No, don't look at me like that,

like you're about to say some pat words about my being around for a long time. I may not be old, but I'm not well. I don't have a lot of years ahead of me."

"I'm sorry," Anne whispered.

"It's all right. The Lord and I have made our peace about my health and I treasure every day I have."

She'd known Margaret was ill, but not how ill. "All the more reason you should be able to spend as much time as you can with Ian."

"I plan to."

Anne stilled. Was Margaret thinking she would move back to the Boston area? She could at the end of the school year. There was a clause in her three-year contract that would allow her to break it for unforeseeable personal reasons.

"I wouldn't be able to move back here until the end of the school year in May." Staying here with Margaret until then should make things easier on Ian. And that's what she wanted, what God wanted, wasn't it? So, why did the whole idea of returning to Boston leave her feeling so defeated?

"Oh, no, I didn't mean for you to totally change your life for Ian." She laughed. "Well, not any more than a child totally changes every parent's life."

Anne's spirits rose. "How? Are you thinking of moving to Paradox Lake?" That could work well for them all.

"No. I was thinking more along the lines of spending holidays together. You have a break at Thanksgiving, right? And a long semester break over Christmas and New Year's. And next summer I just might rent one of those cabins you were telling me Neal and his family have on their campground. A change of pace would be good for me and Maria."

Anne had trouble picturing Margaret in one of the Hazards' rustic cabins. "You're welcome to stay with me. I'm renting my grandmother's old house. Planning to buy it, actually."

"See? I knew you'd be making a sacrifice to come back here."

"But you'll be making a bigger sacrifice letting Ian come home with me. He's your only grandson."

"Then let me be his grandmother." The older woman's voice shook. "I was the one who suggested that Reenie and Rob name you and not me as Ian's guardian."

Warmth filled Anne that Margaret would think so highly of her. But she couldn't help feeling the older woman's confidence in her was misplaced. She didn't know anything about raising a child.

"What about Rob's parents?" Reenie hadn't talked about them much, but they'd certainly done a good job raising Rob.

Margaret shook her head. "They're nice enough people, but they don't have the deep faith Reenie and Rob shared. The faith they want Ian to know. Rob came to Christ as a young adult, like you did."

Anne released Margaret's hand and pushed back in the chair, resting her head against the back and staring at the ceiling. "I don't think I can do it."

Margaret, Reenie. They were asking too much of her. They expected her to be a spiritual guide for Ian. How could she do that when she couldn't even guide herself? Couldn't decipher God's words to her? She raised her head and caught Margaret's frown.

"You think I'm as horrible as Neal does."

"No, I don't. You're overwrought."

Margaret was right. What was happening to her? She'd spent years building a controlled professional demeanor that kept her feelings hidden until she wanted to share them. Neal had broken that barrier and, now, Margaret was seeing through the crack he'd opened.

"But you frowned."

"Because I don't know how to convince you that you'll be fine. Everything will be fine in time."

"I was just thinking about Ian's welfare. I weighed all the factors in a careful, balanced way and came up with what I thought was the best solution."

"Ian's not a problem you can solve with a mathematical equation."

Margaret sounded just like Neal. Anne searched her face for signs of reprimand. Her expression was as gentle as her voice.

"I know, but I needed an answer and I wasn't getting one. I tackled it the only way I knew how."

"Patience and acceptance. You can't push God's will. Can you accept the blessing He's given you?"

"But I don't know how—"

"No," Margaret interrupted. "That doesn't have anything to do with it. Can you accept that Ian is a blessing?"

"Of course. He's a sweet little boy. Anyone would love him."

"Okay. Then accept your blessing. And if you have qualms about how you're going to care for him and raise him, know that all parents do."

"Neal said that, too."

"I'm not surprised. Would you like for me to pray with you for guidance in giving Ian the home Reenie and Rob wanted him to have?"

Margaret made it seem so much simpler, like Reenie would have.

"Yes, I'd like that. A lot." She moved forward and took Margaret's hand again.

"Lord, please help Anne to find her way in undertaking this new path You are leading her on. I know You will watch over her and guide her to make the right decisions to give Ian the stable, happy home Reenie and Rob wanted him to have. And let me share in the joy of my new extended family. In Your name, amen."

Margaret raised her head. "Feel better?"

"Yes, much." Now, if only she could hang on to those words and use them to reassure herself.

Margaret nodded. "That's all you have to do. Relax, accept, don't try so hard. That's what I've done and it's made such a difference in my life."

Anne shifted in the chair. Margaret had a heavier cross to bear.

Margaret released her hand. "You probably want to go find Neal. I take it you told him what you told me and he didn't agree with your decision."

"Yes. And I said things I shouldn't have." Some of the peace she'd gotten praying with Margaret faded. "But I can't."

"Sure you can. Where is he? Outside walking off his anger? That's what Reenie's father used to do when we had a disagreement."

"No. He's gone. He rented a car and is on his way back to Paradox Lake."

"I'm sorry. I'm sure he'll call when he gets home and you'll work things out. I can tell you and he have something special."

"We'll see." Anne didn't want to disappoint the woman. Margaret probably had expectations that Neal might be a male influence in Ian's future. But right now Anne didn't see much chance of that. For now, the most she could hope for was salvaging their teacher-student relationship and getting through the rest of the semester.

Chapter Twelve

"Hi, Dad," Autumn called as she climbed out of her car and crossed the yard. "Reporting for duty."

Neal handed her a rake, glad for her company to distract him from his thoughts. He certainly could have done the raking himself, but it was a job they had done together every fall since she was a little girl.

"Guess who I saw at the grocery store this morning?"

Anne was the first thought that popped into his mind. But she'd been imbedded there since he'd left Boston.

"Who?"

"Mrs. Donnelly and Mr. Stowe. They were doing their shopping together. I think they're such a cute couple." Autumn raked her leaves into the pile Neal had started. "He said that Dr. Howard isn't back from Boston yet."

She stopped raking and looked at him.

"Oh, yeah?" That was news to him, although he had walked by her office at the college a couple days after he'd gotten home and seen a notice on her door that her office hours for that day had been cancelled. She'd probably stayed to hire a nanny for Ian. He attacked the leaves in front of him with a vengeance.

Autumn raised her eyebrows in the way she did when she thought she was on to something interesting. "Mr. Stowe had been keeping an eye on her house. He said he didn't expect her back until after semester break is over week after next."

A whole week and a half away from work. Maybe the nanny search wasn't as easy as Anne had expected. His rake hit a rock and the vibration of the impact reverberated up the handle. He pictured Anne at Margaret's scooping up Ian and snuggling him to her shoulder. Warmth filled him. He was being as judgmental of Anne as he'd accused her of being of him.

He shrugged. "The things she stayed to help Reenie's mother with must be taking longer than she'd expected." That's what he'd told his folks when he'd showed up in the rental car. That Anne had to stay and help Margaret with some things. He hadn't said anything about Ian. He didn't think it was his place to, especially since Anne was leaving the orphaned boy in Boston with Margaret. And he didn't trust himself not to lose his temper telling them about Ian.

"Oh. You'd said the other night when I called that you were working on your independent study course. So, I thought you'd talked with Dr. Howard."

Neal squatted and pulled the rock he'd hit from the ground and tossed it toward the gravel road that ran past the house to the camp lodge. "No. Gary Spear, the Green Spaces project manager for the birthing center, called me. He'd gotten my reports on potential solar energy contractors from Anne and wanted me to get more details on a couple of the companies."

"I see."

He wasn't sure what she saw, but his gut told him it was more than he wanted her to see. What was it with the women in his family that they knew his mind—or thought they knew his mind—before he did? While he was having trouble forgiving Anne for abandoning Ian, a part of him had hoped she would have contacted him by now about school, if nothing else.

"So what are you up to for the break?"

"I've scheduled some more hours at the nursing home and I babysat for Jamie last night while she was at choir practice."

Had Jamie heard from Anne? Probably, but he wasn't going to ask Autumn.

"She's having a party for Opal's fifth birthday on Saturday and you're invited."

"Jamie's not having a kid's party for her?"

"She is, sort of. She told Opal she could invite anyone she wanted, figuring she'd want her friends from preschool, which she did. But she also wanted to invite you and me and Aunt Jinx and Drew and all of the counselors from last summer's camp."

"Sounds like Opal. So Jamie is giving a party for hundreds?"

"Not quite. Jamie convinced Opal that the counselors probably wouldn't be able to come since most of them don't live near here."

"What time is the party?"

"Two. Do you want to go toy shopping together?"

"Sure. That's something we haven't done in a while. As long as you don't beg me to get you a toy, too."

"I think I can restrain myself."

Neal resumed his raking. Maybe he'd pick up a little toy for Ian, too. A truck or tractor. He could mail it to Margaret. She wouldn't have to tell Ian it was from him. He didn't want to confuse the little guy since it wasn't like he was going to have any part in the boy's life.

"Do you think he'll be okay?" Anne glanced over at Ian seated on the floor behind Jamie stacking wood blocks, aided by Jamie's seven-year-old daughter, Rose.

"He'll be fine with the other kids," Jamie said. "You'll only be gone a minute or two. And I do have some experience with toddlers."

"I know." Anne checked on Ian again. He wasn't paying a bit of attention to her.

"If you want, I'll run over to your house and get the napkins and you can supervise the melee here. I was the one who forgot to pick them up when I was getting the party stuff in Ticonderoga. Where are they?"

Anne surveyed the roomful of kids. Jamie's three and most of Opal's preschool class. "No. You're not escaping that easily. And you're right. I should be able to leave him long enough to go next door and back. The last thing I want to be is a helicopter parent."

To Anne's surprise, the word *parent* rolled off her tongue easily.

"I don't think you need to worry about that yet. Ian is only three. Kids that age need quite a bit of hovering."

"I'll be right back."

"Thanks again for picking up the napkins."

"No problem. I was birthday present shopping anyway."

Anne hurried out of the house and across the yard to her place. She and Ian had had a great time at the supercenter in Ticonderoga yesterday. He seemed to understand that the toys she bought were for the birthday party and seemed perfectly content with the crayons and paper she'd gotten him. After a kid's meal from the fast-food restaurant, he'd fallen asleep in the car and she'd been able to get him changed into his pajamas and into bed without him fully waking up.

Day one as a single parent done.

She gave her door a push with her shoulder. The damp fall weather was making it stick. As she picked up the napkins from the kitchen counter, the house phone rang. For a moment, she weighed whether to answer it. No one called her on that phone. Except Mr. Stowe, and he knew she was going to be at Opal's party. She'd told him yesterday morning when he'd stopped by to look at her sticky door and proclaimed it would contract as soon as the temperature dropped a few more degrees and be fine.

She couldn't ignore the insistent ring. "Hello," she answered.

"May I speak with Anne Howard?"

"This is she."

The woman at the other end of the line identified herself as the assistant manager at the supercenter. "You left your debit card at the checkout yesterday. Since there was only one Anne Howard listed in the local online white pages, I took the chance that this was your number."

"Thank you. I didn't realize I hadn't put it back in my wallet." She was never that careless. But Ian had been fussy waiting on line to check out and that must have distracted her.

"You're welcome. You can pick it up at the customer service desk."

"I'll stop by tomorrow."

"Have a nice day." The store manager hung up.

How nice of the manager to call. Back home in Boston—no, this was home, hers and Ian's, for now—once, she'd discovered the card missing, she would have had to retrace her steps to try to locate it.

Anne grabbed the napkins and walked back to Jamie's house. An unfamiliar car was parked in the driveway. Must be another one of Opal's school friends had arrived. She let herself in the kitchen door and followed the cacophony of voices through the dining room to the living room, anxious to check on Ian. Jamie had said he'd be fine, and she was sure he was, but all of the kids were older, and they were pretty noisy.

The scene in the living room stopped her dead in the doorway. Opal had Neal by the hand and was dragging him around the room to meet all of her friends. He must have come with whomever had driven the car she'd seen in the driveway. A date?

Anne squeezed the napkins she should have left in the kitchen. What did it matter? They weren't anything more than friends. If even that anymore. *No!* He was her student. She didn't know or care who her other students were dating.

"And this is my new friend Ian. He lives with Anne now. I think she's his aunt or something."

Anne held her breath, waiting for Neal's reaction. She was allowing the situation to affect her far more than she should.

Ian looked up at the sound of his name.

A muscle worked in Neal's jaw.

The toddler stood and studied Neal. "I know who you are. You're Nal." He grinned up at Neal.

"No, he's not," Opal corrected. "He's Neal."

Ian scrunched his face. "N…N…Ne-al." He clapped his hands.

Neal grinned. "That's right, buddy. How's my guy?" He picked Ian up and raised him above his head.

"Nee Nee," Ian called across the room.

Neal jerked his head toward her and he drilled her with his gaze. She released her breath and gulped another.

He lowered Ian to the floor, keeping his eyes on her the entire time.

Ian said something to Neal and grabbed his hand. They were crossing the room. To her. Anne looked around for Jamie. She hadn't said anything about

Neal coming to the party. Of course, why woul◌ she have? Anne hadn't said anything to her abou◌ what had happened in Boston. It was Anne who'◌ assumed the party was only for kids.

"Dr. Howard. I didn't know you were back.◌ Autumn came up beside her a second before Nea◌ and Ian reached her.

Call her a coward, but Anne was glad she wasn◌ facing Neal alone.

"You're not the only one."

His harsh tone grated on every raw nerve in he◌ body.

"Nee Nee." Ian vied for her attention.

She dragged her gaze from Neal's and focuse◌ on the little boy.

"Ne-al. At the party."

"Yes. I see."

"Who's that?" Ian pointed at Autumn.

Neal spoke first. "That's my big girl, Autumn.

"And who are you?" Autumn glanced from Nea◌ to Anne to Ian, her expression open with questior◌

"Ian," he answered as if that said it all.

Autumn and Neal turned to Anne in a synchro◌ nized movement.

Her mouth went dry. She swallowed and tried t◌ find her voice. "Ian is my, my—"

The set of Neal's jaw challenged her to finisl◌ her sentence.

"Ian is my ward."

Neal's countenance darkened and Autumn looked puzzled.

"My friend Reenie's son. My godchild. He's living with me now."

Neal raised an eyebrow.

"I'm so sorry." Autumn wound a strand of her long blond hair around her finger. "About your friend, I mean. Not about Ian. Dad didn't say anything."

And he still wasn't saying anything. Neal stood expressionless, his hands jammed in the front pockets of his jeans.

Autumn released her hair. "I'm going to go see if Jamie needs any help in the kitchen. I think it's cake time."

She disappeared into the other room, leaving Anne alone with Neal and ten or twelve kids.

"Cake. Ian likes cake."

Anne wasn't a big fan of cake, but she liked this cake if it was going to be served right now and help her avoid a face-to-face with Neal.

"Good. What do you say we go see if Jamie needs more help?"

Ian nodded. "Ne-al help?"

"No, bud. Not this time. You and Aunt Annie can handle it all on your own."

He was dismissing her. Not that she wanted to stick around and talk with him. But who did he think he was, after his assurances that she had

people in Paradox to help her with Ian? Peopl
who included him. She grabbed Ian's hand. Sh
was in control. Hadn't her parents taught her to b
self-sufficient so they could spend as little time a
possible with her? And Michael had groomed he
to be in charge.

Ian yanked his hand back. "No." He stomped hi
foot. "Ne-al help."

"No, I'm sorry, but Neal said he can't help thi
time." She looked directly at Neal, challenging hin
to try to say differently.

He matched her stare, but said nothing.

She took Ian's hand again. His face crumple
and he threw himself on the floor, screaming an
kicking. The other kids circled around.

"What's wrong with him?" Opal asked.

Anne spared the birthday girl a glance.

"He's having a temper tantrum," her older sis
ter, Rose, answered. "Like you used to when yo
were a baby."

"I did not. Mommy!" Opal added her scream t
Ian's. "Rose is being mean to me. On my birthday.

Any thread of control Anne had, or thought she'
had, was frayed to the breaking point. She had n
trouble managing a multinational corporation. Bu
two preschoolers had her paralyzed.

"Rose Elizabeth." Jamie stormed into the livin
room. "Are you picking on your sister?"

"No," Rose said from her lofty two-years-olde

position. "I just said that she used to have temper tantrums like Ian when she was a baby."

"Go and help Autumn with the birthday cake in the kitchen." Jamie pointed toward the doorway. "Opal, tell your friends that it's time to have cake."

Opal started to open her mouth to shout over Ian's continuing screams.

Jamie shook her head no. "Walk around and tell them."

Opal pushed out her lower lip, but did as her mother had told her, rounding up her friends and leading them to the dining room.

Jamie looked down at Ian, who was still screaming and flailing, and then over at Anne and Neal. "I guess Ian's not having cake. I only give cake to little boys who aren't crying."

When Ian screamed louder, Anne bent to pick him up. Ian slapped her hand and Anne stepped back.

"Are you having cake, Neal?" Jamie asked in a sugar-sweet voice.

Neal smirked. He smirked! And stepped over Ian. "I sure am. I'm not crying."

Anne couldn't believe the two of them.

"How about you, Aunt Annie?"

Was Neal mocking her or was she being overly sensitive? Whatever, she'd certainly lost any control she might have had over the situation.

"You're not crying," Jamie added.

Ian stopped kicking his feet. He sat up and sniffled. "Ian not crying." He hiccuped and raised his watery gaze to Neal.

Defeat engulfed Anne. She'd been right. She didn't know anything about being a parent.

Jamie went ahead into the dining room as Ian slid his warm little hand in Anne's.

"Autumn used to have terrible tantrums when she was Ian's age," Neal said as if sharing a great confidence. "But we both got over them. Mom set me straight. As soon as I stopped paying attention to them, she stopped. Like Ian did."

His earnest reassurance relieved some of her self-doubt. "But how do you know when to ignore a behavior?" And when you're ignoring the child, as her parents had too often ignored her.

Neal placed his hand on her shoulder. "It'll come with time."

His touch and words calmed the butterflies of self-doubt in her stomach. But now it churned with another more disturbing feeling.

"Or you can ask me." He flashed her a grin that wrapped around her heart.

A much more disturbing feeling.

"Lose your way?" Jamie asked as Neal and Anne entered the dining room with Ian.

The other children were all seated around the

table. A double layer chocolate cake blazing with five candles sat in front of Opal.

"We were ready to start singing without you," Rose informed them.

Anne helped Ian into the booster seat Jamie had put in one of the chairs. Her obvious concern about Ian when he'd thrown his tantrum and the loving expression on her face now drove out the last bit of anger Neal had felt toward her. She'd be a good mother to Ian, like he and Margaret had agreed. All she'd needed was some encouragement. Encouragement she must have gotten from Margaret, since he'd fallen a little short in that area.

Neal hung back by the doorway, reluctant to join the group in their boisterous, if off-key, rendition of "Happy Birthday." Jamie's teasing and the enjoyment he'd gotten from watching Anne get Ian situated made him stop and put some distance between him and them. Had he just offered to help Anne with Ian? He looked around the table at the kids wriggling and fidgeting in anticipation of having cake and opening Opal's gifts.

His gaze passed over Anne and settled on Autumn standing next to the birthday girl. He'd already done preschool and birthday parties. It was time for him to start living his life for himself. Wasn't it?

"Make a wish and blow out the candles," Jamie said.

Opal puffed out her cheeks and blew. When the

last candle sputtered out, everyone clapped. Neal loudest of all.

Jamie helped Opal cut the cake and Autumn passed the pieces out to everyone.

"Ne-al. Ne-al." Ian patted the table next to him. "Cake."

Autumn raised a plate to him. "We can squeeze you in here."

Neal walked around the table to Autumn and took the piece of cake she'd offered.

"Do you want a chair?" Jamie asked.

"No, I'm fine."

"Choc-it cake." Ian raised his frosting-smeared face to him.

Who was he kidding? He wasn't fine. And if he didn't keep his distance from Ian and Anne, he might never be fine again.

Chapter Thirteen

Neal sat alone at the far left end of the polished maple pew lost in thoughts that didn't exactly put him in the frame of mind for worship. He was almost glad that Autumn had pulled a Sunday morning shift at the nursing home and couldn't come to church with him and Mom and Dad. He glanced over his shoulder to the vestibule where they were cheerfully fulfilling their duties as this morning's greeters and hoped they didn't point his sister and Drew in his direction when they arrived. If they came. Isabelle had been sick yesterday. So maybe they'd stay home with her.

He didn't know why he'd turned so antisocial. He hadn't had a bad week. In the larger scheme of things, it had been a good week. With no classes, he'd had time to catch up on several wiring jobs he'd lined up. But it gnawed at him that Anne had "reassigned" his work study supervision to Gary

Speer, as the project manager had put it to Neal in his email. Neal rested his head in his hands. And that gnawing bothered him. He'd decided at Opal's party that he needed to keep his distance from Anne. He should be glad she was obliging him.

"It's so good to see you again." His mother's greeting carried into the sanctuary. He heard a soft murmur of a reply that sounded a lot like Anne. But Anne hadn't attended Community Church in several weeks.

"Ne-al!" Ian's exclamation echoed off the sanctuary's vaulted wood ceiling.

Neal snapped his head up to see Ian charging down the center aisle with Anne close on his heels. Most of the congregation looked their way, more than a few of them smiling. He could see the local grapevine sending out its tentacles already.

She caught up with Ian at the other end of Neal's pew. "We're in church," Anne admonished him in a loud whisper.

"I know," he said, eluding her grasp and making a beeline down the pew to Neal. "Sit with Ne-al."

Ian scrambled up on Neal's lap and gave Anne a beatific smile that challenged her to say otherwise.

She stood rigid, hands on hips and glared at the toddler. It took everything Neal had not to laugh at the standoff.

"Sit," Ian said. "Peese."

Anne's demeanor softened. "Do you mind?"

"No." Despite the stares of the congregation and intentions to keep his distance from Anne and Ian, he didn't mind at all.

Anne sat and placed her handbag on the pew between her and Neal. She'd decided to make Community Church her home church before she and Neal had gone to Margaret's. Pastor Joel's sympathy call early last week when she was still in Sudbury had chipped away at the foolish change of mind she'd contemplated after her and Neal's argument. The pastor's wife's warm welcoming of Ian into the day care/preschool program she directed at the church had clinched her return to Community. No reason to let her and Neal's relationship or, more precisely, nonrelationship, stop her and Ian from being part of the church community she felt most comfortable with.

She glanced at Ian snuggled against Neal's chest sucking his thumb and resisted both the impulse to gently pull Ian's thumb from his mouth and to look directly at Neal.

Ian caught her look and pulled his thumb out himself. "Sing book."

"He means the hymnal." Neal pointed at the book rack on the back of the pew in front of them.

She knew that. So far, the only communication problem she and Ian had had was the tantrum at

Opal's party last Saturday. Anne lifted a hymnal from the rack.

"Ribbons. Ian show you." He climbed from Neal's lap to the floor, opened the hymnal and started putting the place marker ribbons on random pages.

"Whoa." Neal reached over and stopped. "How about you let Aunt Annie turn to the right song page and then you can mark them with the ribbons?"

"Okay."

Anne's heart softened. Neal hadn't been criticizing her lack of experience with children. She had to stop being defensive. Raising Ian wasn't a competition.

Ian placed the last ribbon.

"All done," Anne said.

He snapped the book shut with a bam.

Neal held up a second hymnal. "Want to help me?"

"Nope."

Anne smiled as Ian climbed back on Neal's lap.

"How am I going to sing the songs without a song book?"

"Share with Nee Nee." Ian pulled the hymnal from Anne's lap to Neal's.

Anne waited for Neal's response. *There was something a touch too intimate about sharing a hymnal.*

"But there are enough books for both of us to have one."

"No," Ian insisted. "At 'kool, Miss Jenfer says we have to share."

"She does, does she? You're right. Better not argue with the teacher, right, Aunt Annie?"

Before she could answer, the choir director finished the prelude. She struck a chord on the piano, and the choir began walking down the aisle, voices raised in song.

Neal placed the second hymnal on the seat to his far side and lowered Ian to the floor in front of him. He flipped open the marked song book and offered her the right-hand side to hold, closing the distance she'd put between them. As his rich baritone joined the choir voices, the harmony of the praise washed over her and she allowed herself to enjoy the fellowship of the moment.

When the song ended, Anne came back to reality with a start, released the hymnal as if it were a hot potato and put as much space between her and Neal as she could without being too obvious in her action. Ian climbed up on the pew and situated himself in the space, allowing her to regain some of her equilibrium.

The little boy patted her leg. "Story."

"Shh, I can't read you a story right now. We're going to say a prayer." She bowed her head and folded her hands, hoping he'd follow suit.

"No, story." He pointed to the front of the church.

He couldn't be talking about the sermon. He wasn't quite three.

"Opal said." His voice rose.

Anne's stomach dropped. He wasn't going to have a trantrum, was he? Not here in church. Not on their first Sunday.

Pastor Joel finished the prayer and the choir rose for a praise song. Ian swung his little legs back and forth to the rhythm of the song and Anne relaxed.

The choir members returned to their seats.

"Story now." Several people in the pews ahead of them turned at Ian's louder insistence. A couple of them smiled. A couple others didn't.

Anne debated whether she should take Ian out into the vestibule or whether that would interrupt service more. She was not going to turn to Neal for help. She should be able to handle something as simple as Ian talking in church.

Pastor Joel stepped down from the lectern. And walked to the center of the steps to the altar.

"Nee Nee." In Anne's ears her name echoed off the walls and ceiling.

The pastor looked out at them and she wanted to melt to the floor under the pew.

"I'd like all the children to join me for a story," he said.

"See, Nee Nee. Story. Opal said."

The bands constricting her lungs unwound. "Yes. A story." Her words whooshed out.

Opal and Rose trooped down the aisle and stopped at the end of their pew. "Mommy said Ian can come with us," Rose said.

"Do you want to go with the girls?"

"No. Nee Nee and Neal. Story."

None of the other parents were with the children making their way down front.

"It's been a while," Neal said, "but I can handle this if you want me to."

Anne could have hugged him for the offer. Except they were in church. And she shouldn't be thinking about hugging Neal in church or anywhere else. She'd planned to quietly attend service as she had the other times she'd visited Hazardtown Community Church before she'd made her decision to join its fellowship. She'd never imagined something so simple could be so difficult.

Neal rose and took Ian's hand and motioned the girls to go ahead. "Come on, bud."

Ian hesitated. Anne grasped the back of the pew in front of her with her right hand. After all of his vocal anticipation of the story, he wasn't going to go with Neal to hear it?

"Nee Nee, too."

"I think you'd better come." Neal lifted his chin toward the front of the church where Pastor Joel and the other children appeared to be waiting for them.

Anne stood and took Ian's other hand and they walked up the side aisle with, she was sure, every eye in the church on them. From the knowing smiles on the faces of some of the congregants, she could imagine the false family picture the three of them must be portraying.

But she couldn't muster the embarrassment she should be feeling, despite her mother's niggling voice in the back of her head. *Watch your actions, don't give anyone a reason to gossip about you.* There would be time to untangle the grapevine later. She and Ian *were* a family. And people could talk all they wanted about that.

Edna Donnelly accosted Neal and Anne on their way out of the sanctuary after service. That was the only way Neal could describe his former English teacher's situating herself between them and the line of people filing out by Pastor Joel. Accosted in a good way, if there was such a thing.

"Annie, I'm so glad you're joining us here at Community."

Anne's cheeks flushed as the well-meaning older woman's loud greeting filled the church and vestibule and probably carried downstairs to the church hall, as well.

"Mrs. Donnelly. Good to see you again."

"And this must be Ian." She ruffled his red curls

and he ducked behind Anne. "Harry told me all about him."

The older woman's proclamation pricked Neal. Anne's landlord, Harry Stowe, knew all about Ian? When Anne hadn't seen fit to even let him know she'd returned from Sudbury, let alone that she'd changed her mind about taking the toddler? Neal had found out completely by accident. He crumpled his bulletin and tossed it in the wastebasket. Was he jealous of an eighty-year-old man?

"Are you coming, Neal?" Mrs. Donnelly asked. "You're holding up the line."

Neal glanced over his shoulder and gave the people behind them an apologetic smile.

The four of them made their way to the pastor.

Pastor Joel took Mrs. Donnelly's hand in his. "Good morning. Always good to see you."

"You, too. I especially enjoyed the Scripture reading today. Psalm 34:4 is one of my favorites. 'I sought the Lord, and he answered me; he delivered me from all my fears.'" She repeated it from memory. "I relied on that verse when I lost my husband and again when my grandson was wounded in Afghanistan. Got me through both times."

"I'm glad to hear that. I wish more people would rely on His guidance."

Pastor Joel released Mrs. Donnelly's hand and reached for Anne's. "Anne, I'm so glad you decided to join us."

She stepped forward and extended her hand but didn't meet the minister's gaze.

Neal watched with interest. What had unsettled her? Did she expect Joel to criticize Ian's behavior? Neal had a feeling that her parents were very critical. That would explain a lot of her drive for success. If she thought Pastor Joel would judge her like that, she didn't know him at all.

"And who is this guy?" Pastor Joel smiled down at Ian.

"This is my… This is Ian."

"Hi, Ian. Did you enjoy the Bible story?"

He nodded his answer. "Neal, too."

"I could tell," Joel said with exaggerated seriousness. "Do you know that that's the first time Neal has come forward for the story?"

"I bring him," Ian chimed.

"Yes, and you can bring him again anytime you want. Him and…" Pastor Joel hesitated and glanced over at Anne, unsure how to address her to Ian.

"Nee Nee," Ian offered.

Neal interpreted. "Aunt Annie."

The corner of Joel's mouth quirked up, belying his otherwise solemn expression. And Anne's already pink cheeks went crimson.

"Neal." Pastor Joel shook his hand as Anne attempted to hustle Ian through the vestibule to the door. "I appreciate the evangelism."

Joel nodded toward Anne, who'd almost made

it to the door before Mrs. Donnelly had grabbed her arm.

"I had nothing to do with it," Neal said.

Pastor Joel ignored his protest. "I hear Anne's joined your Singles Plus group, too."

It wasn't his group. He was just the leader for the current Bible study module.

"She's only come once. Several weeks ago. *With Jamie*," he emphasized.

"From the looks of things, I'm sure you can get her to come back."

"I'll talk with Jamie."

"You do that." Pastor Joel turned to the next person in line.

Did that really just happen? Pastor Joel matchmaking? Neal expected it of some of the other church members, but not his pastor and friend. He strode to the door before remembering that he'd come with Mom and Dad. They'd be downstairs in the church hall. He shouldn't leave without telling them, even though having to report in struck him as juvenile. Otherwise, Mom and Dad would be looking for him when they were ready to leave.

He trudged down the stairs and pasted a smile on his face. Maybe he could catch one of them quickly and avoid having to talk with anyone. The walk home in the brisk November air would do him good. Help him clear his mind.

"There you are," Mrs. Donnelly called as he entered the hall. "We saved you a place." She motioned to the table where, from the pained smile on Anne's face, she held Anne and Ian captive, well guarded by Mr. Stowe and several of the church's evangelism committee. His heart went out to Anne in sympathy.

Correct that. Ian was in his glory shoveling in cake and chattering away to Mr. Stowe, who was nodding thoughtfully, as if carefully contemplating each of the boy's words. More likely he had his hearing aid turned down and wasn't hearing most of what Ian was saying.

Neal scanned the room for his parents and found his mother passing by her usual coffee hour group and making a beeline for Mrs. Donnelly's table. His dad was nowhere in sight. Mom placed her coffee cup on the table next to Anne. She was up to something. He could tell by the glint in her eyes. He motioned to her that he was leaving. Either she didn't see him or was ignoring him. He debated whether it was the latter and he should just go ahead and leave.

"Ne-al."

Ian's call to him resolved the debate. No way he could slip out now. He dragged himself over.

"I'm glad I found you," his mother said.

Like she hadn't just seen him standing across the room motioning to her. Yep, she was up to something, and a sinking feeling in his stomach said that something had to do with Anne and Ian.

"I was just telling Anne that your father has gone over to the parsonage with the building committee to take a look at the damage to the roof from last week's hail. I don't know how long they'll be."

"That's okay. I thought I'd walk home."

His mother looked at his cotton dress shirt. "You don't have a jacket."

Across the table from him, Anne took an intense interest in her coffee.

"Here, take my coffee." His mother pointed to the space next to Anne. "I'll go and get another. They just put out Karen Hill's cheesecake cookies."

Neal didn't recall his mother being such a big fan of cheesecake. He walked around the table and slid into the place next to her.

Anne turned to him. "That's one of the reasons I've put some miles between my mother and me."

More unsolicited advice on how he should have lived his life? He gripped the insulated paper cup and hot coffee spilled over on his hand and the table.

Anne wiped the table with her napkin. "I was teasing."

He should have known that. Her deprecating sense of humor was one of the many things he'd always liked about Annie, along with the way her soft hair framed her delicate features, her perfect fair skin that pinked at the least suggestion of embarrassment, her expressive brown eyes that a man could lose himself in and…

Get ahold of yourself, Hazard. You're not a junior in high school anymore and she's not little Annie O'Connor. She's Anne Howard. And Anne Howard was someone very different from straightforward Annie, as her actions with Ian had shown him.

To cover himself, Neal released an exaggerated sigh. "But with Emily married and Autumn off in her own apartment, Mom would have no one to mother. Who knows what she'd resort to?"

"Neal Theodore Hazard." His mother came up behind him. "I know you're talking about me. And I know our Annie doesn't believe a word of it."

He and Anne exchanged a quick glance. When had she become *our* Annie?

"Anyway, Annie said she'd give us a ride home, so we don't have to wait around for your dad."

Anne choked on her coffee.

While Neal was sure Anne had agreed to drive Mom home as she'd said, he'd guess she'd failed to mention to Anne that he'd come with his parents.

"These cookies are really good. Want one?" His mother held her paper plate out to Anne.

"No, thanks."

Neal gulped his coffee. His mother was matchmaking. She'd been hinting for more grandchildren for years, but to be this overt was unlike her.

"Nee Nee." Ian pushed his plate between him and Anne.

He must have finished his talk with Mr. Stowe.

"More cake?"

"No, sweetie, I think you've had enough."

The corners of the boy's mouth turned down.

"And we have to drive Neal home." Anne's eyes pleaded with him for support.

"And my mother."

Ian's chin quivered when he heard the word *mother*.

Not the best choice of words.

"You can call me Grandma Mary, like Rose and Opal and the other kids do."

"I know Opal," Ian said.

Mom to the rescue. Neal had to be thankful for her help defusing a possible meltdown, but he was still uneasy with the direction his mother was taking.

Ian's eyes brightened. "Ian has a grandma."

"And what a lucky grandma she is to have a big boy like you. I have two granddaughters, Autumn and baby Isabelle."

"Ne-al's big girl?"

"Right. How did you know?"

"Opal's birthday party."

"Aren't you a smart guy to remember?"

Ian grinned.

"If you're done with your coffee," Mary said, "why don't you and Anne take Ian out to the car? I remember how much time it used to take me to get Autumn all strapped into her car seat when she was that age."

"Ian has a big-boy seat." He bounced on the balls of his feet.

"His grandmother Margaret got it for him. His old one was…" Anne twisted and untwisted her coffee-stained napkin. "He needed a new one."

Mary Hazard nodded, compassion framing her expression. "I'm going to call Ted and let him know we're leaving. I'll be right out."

Anne helped Ian into his jacket and Neal walked them out of the hall in what felt to him like a replay of their trek down the church aisle for the Bible story.

"I need to stop in the preschool room and pick up my gloves. I left them there Friday."

"Sure, you're the driver."

When they reached the door to the classroom, Ian dug in his heels and tugged at Anne's hand. "No 'kool. I stay with Nee Nee."

"We just have to go in for a minute. You can show Neal your cubby."

"No." He stomped his foot. "No 'kool."

A memory clicked in Neal's head. Ian had said something about school and Miss Jennifer in church. Neal hadn't connected it with Pastor Joel's wife, Jennifer, and the Community Church preschool and day care. He'd thought Ian was talking about his preschool in Sudbury.

"Do you mind staying here in the hall with him?" Anne asked. "I don't know what's gotten into him. He was fine here all week."

Anne had brought Ian to day care, even though the college had been closed for the week? The concern on Anne's face as she looked at Ian stopped Neal's budding anger. It wasn't as if he knew Anne's every move, what she may have had to do this past week, why she might have needed day care.

"No problem," he said.

"I'll be right back," she reassured Ian. "Neal will stay with you."

"Okay." Ian wrapped his arm around Neal's leg and stuck his thumb in his mouth.

The grip on his leg relaxed.

"Miss Jenfer." Ian hid behind Neal and peeked around at the pastor's wife.

She waved and walked over. "Ian, I'm happy to see you at church this morning."

Ian came out from behind Neal and went to her. He gave her a shy smile.

Whatever problem he'd had with day care didn't appear to extend to Jennifer.

"Neal." Ian pointed.

"Yes, I'm glad to see him, too."

"We take Neal home."

"Is that right?" Jennifer's eyes sparkled.

Neal shifted his weight to his other foot. She'd better not be thinking about teaming up with her husband on matchmaking because they'd both be sorely disappointed by the results.

Her lips curved up.

Sure she was. But it wasn't going to work. He and Anne wanted different things. They didn't have anything in common anymore. All they'd ever had in common was their high school science team.

"Dad has some building-committee business. Anne's giving Mom and me a ride home."

"I see."

Why did everyone keep saying that? If what they were seeing was him and Anne as a couple, they needed their vision checked. If he were looking for a relationship, which he wasn't certain he was, what he wanted was a child-free relationship.

"Got them." Anne held up the black leather driving gloves as she stepped from the classroom into the hall. "Jennifer, hi!"

"I saw Ian and Neal." Jennifer's eyes sparkled again. "And I thought I'd catch you and thank you again for all of the time you spent helping out at day care this week. It was a lifesaver with my assistant being out sick most of the days."

"Don't thank me," Anne said. "Ian and I got as

much out of our time as you did. I think he'll adjust much better to coming this week without me."

"See you tomorrow morning, then. And you, too, Ian. You all have a nice afternoon." Jennifer looked directly at Neal.

Neal strained to return her seemingly innocuous smile. Jennifer obviously thought they were spending the day together. Which they weren't. Unless his mother decided to invite them to dinner. Which he fervently hoped she wouldn't.

"Neal?" Anne broke into his thoughts. "Your mom will be waiting."

He blinked her into focus, and the questioning tilt of her tentative smile made his heart do a double somersault.

Yes, he hoped his mom didn't invite Anne to stay. He needed some time alone to rebuild his wall of reasons why they couldn't be together. Because right now he couldn't remember any of them.

Chapter Fourteen

Anne steeled herself not to shiver in the chilly fifty-eight-degree temperature of the birthing center construction trailer while she and Ray Newcomb, the representative from GoSolar, waited for Neal.

What had prompted her to wear a dress rather than one of her wool suits? Habit. Michael had always encouraged her to balance what he called her male business mind with femininity. Under the desk, she smoothed the soft, silky skirt of the wrap dress. She had warmer outfits that were probably just as feminine as the dress. But they hadn't garnered her as many compliments. To be honest, she wanted to look nice for Neal. She'd thought she'd seen a glimmer of disappointment in his eyes last Sunday when she'd declined his mother's invitation to dinner. She wanted to explore that glimmer.

Ray finished reviewing the meeting agenda and

laid his plans out on the desk. "These trailers sure don't warm up fast, do they?"

He must have seen her shiver. Anne glanced over at the portable electric radiator that was glowing away in a valiant effort to warm the room. The GoSolar representative had worn a flannel shirt over what was probably a long-sleeved T-shirt. She silently chided herself for putting personal—and ungrounded—wants ahead of business practicality.

"Except in the summer," she said.

"You've got that right."

A silence settled over the office. Ray looked toward the door, checked his watch and looked back at the door, seemingly uncomfortable that she'd taken Gary's place in the meeting. That, or he was in a hurry to get the meeting over with, which would be out of character for a salesperson.

Ray checked his watch again.

Neal wasn't late. She mentally jumped to his defense. They were early.

The trailer door opened letting in Neal and a shot of frigid air. He quickly closed the door behind him.

"Anne." He looked from her to the clock and back.

"Gary got tied up with another project in New Hampshire, so I'm sitting in." If Neal was surprised that she was here instead of the project manager as he'd expected, he'd done a good job of hiding it. And of hiding any pleasure at seeing her here. "This is Ray Newcomb from GoSolar."

"Neal Hazard."

Ray stood and the men shook hands.

Anne bit her lip. She was behaving like the high-school girl with a crush she'd once been. Why had she told Gary he didn't need to let Neal know about the meeting change? Because she'd thought it would be fun to surprise him. How unprofessional could she get? This was a business meeting, not a social engagement.

Neal took the chair next to Ray.

"I really like your ideas," Ray said. "They weren't at all what I'd expected from a college freshman. Then Gary forwarded your resume and I saw your experience."

"Thanks," Neal said. "I'm very interested in the potential of solar power."

"It shows."

Anne silently told herself that the pride she felt in Neal was nothing more than an instructor's pleasure in a student doing well.

Ray looked across the desk at her almost as an afterthought. "You've reviewed the plans?"

Anne bristled. Of course she'd looked at the plans, and not just because Neal had worked on them as part of his class. Ray must not realize who she was.

"Yes, I like to keep a hand in all of our projects."

Ray gave her a curt, dismissive nod and turned his attention back to Neal.

"Dr. Howard reviewed everything before I submitted the plans to Gary."

Rather than soothing her, Neal's defense left her more ruffled. While she knew she should be appreciative, she resented Neal's thinking he needed to defend her almost as much as she did Ray's dismissal of her authority.

Anne reached over and pointed at the schematics. "I had Gary make a slight change here to your plans."

Neal leaned closer to study the diagram, his eyes bright with interest. Anne warmed at his respect for her knowledge far more than she had at his defense of it. Ray sat back in his seat, arms crossed.

"Yes." Neal nodded. "I'm not an engineer, but as an electrician, I can see how that change in the circuitry will improve the flow."

Anne explained her change to Ray. "It shouldn't make any difference in your bid."

Ray uncrossed his arms. "I'm not an engineer, either, so I'll defer to your expertise."

She reveled in the satisfaction Ray's response gave her and immediately regretted her reaction. *Lord, please forgive me my pride.* The short prayer popped into her head naturally and made her feel more in control of herself and the situation. She smiled.

"Go ahead. Tell us why we should use GoSolar."

Leaning back in her chair, she faced Ray and his presentation, all the while glancing sidewise at Neal, enjoying his intent interest and pointed questions, taking pleasure that she could give him this opportunity.

They did make a good team, like back in high school. But they weren't in high school and she shouldn't read anymore into her pleasure than teamwork. If she didn't watch herself, she'd be drawn into believing the gossip about her and Neal that, after Sunday, was sure to be spreading around town.

Ray finished his presentation and looked to Neal, who turned to Anne.

She hoped he'd caught her slight nod of thanks. Thanks she'd give him verbally once Ray left.

Anne stood and offered her hand over the desk to Ray. "Thank you. As Gary told you, we're taking bids from several solar companies. I have yours." She patted a green folder on the desk. "I'll pass on my and Neal's notes to Gary. It's been a pleasure meeting you."

Ray shook her hand. "Same here." He rolled his copy of the plans and put them in the cardboard tube he'd brought them in.

Anne stepped from the desk to walk him to the door.

Ray stood but didn't move. "Neal, have you got a minute? Like I said, I went over your resume and your references. GoSolar could use you. We're always looking for reputable licensed electricians to do final hookups for us. We can grab a cup of coffee and talk about it."

Anne held her breath waiting for Neal's answer. She'd planned on Neal staying so they could go over Ray's presentation together.

"Sounds good to me. Did you need me to stay for anything?" he asked in what sounded like an afterthought to Anne.

"No, we're done." She kept her voice carefully modulated so her disappointment wouldn't show. "Gary'll give you a call when he has the other solar company presentations scheduled."

"Great."

He grinned and her heart hitched at the pure joy in it. Except the joy was for the work opportunity, not for her.

"We can get coffee at the Corner Café in Ticonderoga. You can follow me over."

"Sounds good." Ray opened the trailer door. "When can I expect to hear something, Dr. Howard?"

"I plan to make my decision by the end of the month."

"Thanks."

After a perfunctory wave, Neal followed Ray out the door.

Anne shivered and picked up the folder with

Ray's quote and stuffed it in her briefcase. She'd look it over in the comfort of her office at the college. *Alone.* What was wrong with her? It wasn't like she and Neal had plans for after the meeting. He hadn't even known she was going to be there.

She snapped the case shut. What was wrong with her was that she couldn't get the picture of Neal and Ian at church story time out of her head. And it didn't help that every day when she dropped Ian off at the church day care, he asked, "See Neal?"

She lifted her camel-hair coat off the coat tree and shrugged it on, taking a moment to luxuriate in the added warmth. This morning, for a split second after Ian had turned his big blue eyes on her and once again asked, "See Neal?" she'd entertained the thought of bringing Ian with her so he could see Neal. Then her business sense had snapped in. She'd braced herself for his disappointment and given him her usual, "Not today, sweetie. Neal's very busy."

She flicked the room heater off. And from the conversation with Ray as they were leaving, Neal was about to get busier. Anne opened the door to a snow globe of fat flakes and a dusting of snow that made everything look fresh and new. Neal had seemed very interested in the prospect of working as an electrician for GoSolar. She hoped he wasn't overextending himself and neglecting his classes. His academic advisor, Jeff Lawler, had said Neal had a spotty attendance record in a couple of required core classes.

She opened her car door and tossed her case across the seat to the passenger side. After all of her qualms about her ability to mother Ian, here she was fretting over Neal like a mom. She turned the car on and put it in Drive. Halfway down the gravel drive to the highway, she hit the brakes.

Money! Neal must need the work. That's why he jumped at the offer Ray had made. It made sense. Neal must have lost business while he was serving in Afghanistan with his reserve unit, and construction in the area was still depressed from the economic recession. He needed to support himself and Autumn while they went to school. Why hadn't she thought of that?

She put the car in Park and grabbed her cell phone.

"Adriene." She addressed the Green Spaces chief financial officer. "I have another scholarship candidate. I know we've traditionally given the scholarships to students entering their junior year, but I have a unique student here at NCCC. He's an older student." She described Neal's situation.

"I'm sure he'll be transferring to Rensselaer Polytechnic Institute once he finishes here and will really need the scholarship assistance then. If you can email me the recommendation form, I'll complete it and send it right back. Thanks. And Happy Thanksgiving to you, too."

Anne ended the call, smiling as she drove the rest of the way to the highway. She'd been so busy since returning from Sudbury, she hadn't given any thought to Thanksgiving next week. She had so much to be thankful for this year. Ian, her position at the college, her new friends in Paradox. God had been good to her. Warmth that had nothing to do with the heat blasting from the dashboard filled her. And she could share her good fortune with Neal.

Neal stared at the words on his laptop screen. He had no motivation to finish this paper, except it was due the day after tomorrow. He'd done the research and what he'd written so far was probably fine. But he had no interest in it. What would he ever use general psychology for? He'd mastered all the psychology he needed raising Autumn. And it wasn't likely he'd need that knowledge again. Except for helping Anne with Ian. He tapped his fingers on the desk. But Ian and Anne weren't his responsibility.

He forced himself to resume his writing, pounding on the keyboard in hopes that getting the paper out of the way would lift the heaviness he couldn't seem to shake.

Footsteps sounded in the hall outside his room, followed by a knock on the door.

His dad pushed the door open. "Sorry to interrupt you, but I could use a hand. Your mother's washing machine is leaking and I want to look at the connections." Ted Hazard shook his head in disgust. "But she's fussing about my back. Thinks I could throw it out again like I did last summer."

"No problem, Dad." Neal was up and across the room in the time it took him to answer. "I'm basically done here."

He followed his father to the basement, where the washing machine stood in a puddle of water.

"Let's have a look." His father plugged in a trouble light and hung it on one of the hooks of his mother's indoor clothesline.

Neal pulled the washer out from the cement wall.

His father squatted and held the light up. "Just what I thought. The drain hose is split. Want to run up to the hardware store with me to get another one?"

Neal rubbed his neck. He should finish his paper and tackle some of the other assignments he'd let pile up. "Sure. Your car or my truck?"

"The car. I want to get gas for your mother while we're in town. She's driving Edna Donnelly up to Saranac for a cardiologist appointment tomorrow."

"Is Mrs. Donnelly okay?"

"Yeah, it's her regular checkup."

Neal followed his father up the stairs.

"Mary," his father shouted from the kitchen to

the living room. "Neal and I are running over to the store to get a hose to fix the washer. Need anything from town?"

"Not that I can think of. Thanks," she called back.

Outside, Neal opened the door to his parents' sedan, lowered himself into the passenger seat and adjusted it back.

"So," his father asked, as he turned from Hazard Cove Road to Route 74, "how was your meeting with the construction manager and the solar guy?"

Neal stretched his legs. "Gary couldn't make it. Some problem on another job."

"Rescheduled, then?"

"No, Anne filled in for Gary."

"Interesting."

Neal ignored the inflection in his father's voice. "She keeps a hand in the business even with her teaching position." Neal didn't know that for a fact, except for the birthing center project in Ticonderoga. But it seemed like Anne.

His dad slowed for the curve into the Village of Schroon Lake. "That's a lot of responsibility. Heading up an international company, teaching at the college and, now, raising little Ian."

"Yeah," Neal agreed. And Anne didn't just teach at the college. She was in charge of the environmental studies program. "Makes me feel like I could be doing a better job of handling my business and my classes."

"School's not going any better?" His dad turned into the combination lumberyard hardware store.

"Not exactly."

"You coming in?" Ted opened the car door.

"No, I'll wait out here for you."

Neal folded his hands behind his head and leaned back on the headrest. Closing his eyes to the glare of the cloudless ice-blue sky, he weighed whether to bring up his doubts about college. After the offer Ray had made him this morning at the café, he was seriously considering ending his college career, such that it was, at the end of the semester. Except what kind of example would that set for Autumn?

He took a deep breath and blew it out. And Anne would be disappointed in him. The truth was that bothered him more than any concerns about Autumn. He had no doubts Autumn would finish her nursing program and probably go on somewhere else after NCCC. She loved it. Like Anne seemed to love her work. He liked his work, too, but he couldn't say the same for most of his college classes.

"Hey, you napping on the job?" His dad opened the truck door and tossed the bag with the washer hose onto the backseat.

"Resting my eyes."

"That's my line."

Neal laughed. Whenever anyone caught his dad

sleeping in his recliner in front of the TV, he always said he was resting his eyes.

"Do you want to talk about it?" his dad asked abruptly when they hit the highway home.

"What do you mean?" Neal said, automatically taking on the defensive bent that had marked his younger relationship with his dad. Old habits died hard.

"It may be none of my business, but something's eating at you."

"Ray Newcomb, the representative from GoSolar, made me an offer I'm hard-pressed to refuse."

Ted scratched his head. "Your school project?"

"No, business. GoSolar would like me to be one of their electrical contractors, hooking up the solar installations."

His father nodded.

"I'd get some travel out of it. They've done projects all up and down the East Coast."

"You want to take the offer."

"Yeah."

"Go for it. Autumn's on her own now for the most part. We'd be here for her when you're traveling. Emily and Drew, too. It's not like when you were deployed two years ago and your Mom and I were in Florida with your grandmother. What's stopping you?"

"College. I'd probably have to can the spring semester. Don't know about the fall one. Ray said he could keep me busy spring through late fall, depending on the weather. But what kind of example does that set for Autumn? My quitting after one semester? And even with you being here, I know how hard it was on Autumn when I was in Afghanistan."

"You sure it's Autumn you're concerned about, not Annie?" Ted hesitated. "And her little guy? Even I couldn't miss the way you looked at them at church last week. Or the way her eyes were on you all though the children's story."

"Not you, too, Dad."

"What?" His father hit a pothole in the road and frowned.

"I'm not blind. I saw everyone smiling when we walked Ian up to the altar steps. On the way out, Pastor Joel thanked me for my 'evangelism' in Anne's decision to join our church. At coffee hour, Mom told Ian he could call her Grandma Mary. Said everyone does. And when Anne stopped by the day care to get her gloves, Jennifer assumed Anne and Ian and I were spending the day together."

"You do make a good-looking family. Like us when you and Emily were small." His father chuckled. "Not that we aren't still a good-looking family."

For what it was worth, Neal glared at his father.

"I call it as I see it. You like Annie."

Neal started to protest.

"Don't argue. It looked to me like Annie doesn't mind you being around, either. If you ask me…"

"Which I didn't." Neal stopped. "Sorry, Dad. No disrespect intended."

"None taken. What I was going to say is that you might want to take her out. See where things go from there."

Neal focused on a stone on the floor mat and shook his head.

"Why not?"

"Ian. He's a great little guy. But I've done the raising-kids thing. When I got back from my tour, I promised myself I'd take some time for me. Go back to school." He shrugged. "You know. That plan doesn't include starting over with kids, which I'd be doing if Anne and I get together."

"And how's that plan going?" his father challenged him. "Doesn't sound like you're getting what you expected out of your college classes."

He met his father's gaze. "No, I'm not." Saying it aloud felt unexpectedly good, like a weight had been lifted off his chest.

"Maybe you should reconsider my advice."

What was his father talking about?

"As far as I can see, you're the only one holding you to that plan. Give it up to God. He may have a better plan for you, one that has room for Annie and Ian."

"Yeah." A picture of Anne smoothing Ian's red

curls from his forehead flashed in his head, unleashing an unexpected flow of warmth that he had no strength to fight. "I'll do that."

Chapter Fifteen

"Come on. Please pick up." Anne tapped her foot in time to the ringing phone.

"Hello," Jamie said breathlessly.

"Jamie. I'm so glad you're home. I'm in a jam, and I need a big favor. I'd completely forgotten about the zoning board meeting tonight at the town hall until the alert sounded on my phone. The local attorney Green Spaces hired to represent us said the meeting is just a formality, but I think I should be there. Is there any chance you could watch Ian for me?"

Jamie hesitated and Anne's heart sank. She was imposing, and Jamie was probably too polite to say so. How had she forgotten the meeting? It had been scheduled for weeks, since before Ian came into her life. She glanced at him seated on the floor near her feet, head bent, concentrating on putting together the ten pieces of his wooden fire truck puzzle. He turned and smiled up at her and her heart swelled with love.

"I'm sorry." Jamie's voice drew her back to the phone. "I was on my way out to choir practice with Emily, for the Christmas concert. It's the first one."

"I understand." Anne checked her watch. She'd have to try to get ahold of the attorney.

"Wait. Mary is watching my kids and Isabelle. Drew is down in New York City for a couple of days. I'm sure she won't mind watching Ian, too, if you think he'll be comfortable with her."

If Neal was going to be there, Ian would be just fine. But she wasn't going to say that. Jamie might get the wrong idea, like Pastor Joel's wife. From some of the things Jennifer had said to Anne this week when she'd picked up Ian, it was apparent Jennifer thought she and Neal were a couple. Anne knew she should have set her straight, but she hadn't. Nor did she want to delve into why she'd kept silent.

"Ian met Mary at church the other Sunday. She even told him to call her Grandma Mary, that all of the kids do."

"Yeah," Jamie confirmed. "Mine do, from Autumn and from the past two summers when I worked as the camp nurse. Mary helps out a lot. She loves kids."

Anne waffled. She needed to make this meeting, but she didn't want to impose. It was her own fault she hadn't made arrangements. "You don't think she'll mind?"

"I know she won't mind. But the choir director will if Emily and I are late to practice. She's a stickler for punctuality."

"Sorry. I'll grab Ian's backpack. I have it packed for day care tomorrow. And we'll be right out."

Anne hung up and checked her watch again. She'd have just enough time to do her hair and touch up her makeup before she had to leave. She picked up the backpack and headed toward the door.

"Nee Nee?"

The high-pitched question stopped her in her tracks. *Ian!* She'd forgotten Ian. Anne could imagine the laugh Jamie would have gotten out of her delivering the bag without the baby.

"Sweetie, Mo…" Anne stopped. She'd almost called herself Mommy. "Aunt Annie," she corrected herself, "has to go to a meeting tonight. Jamie is going to take you with Rose and Opal to play at Mrs. Hazard's house until I'm done. Doesn't that sound like fun?"

His brow wrinkled.

"You remember. Mrs. Hazard talked to you at church." Anne took a breath. "Neal's mommy." She almost laughed at her words. It sounded like she was talking about one of Ian's playmates.

"Okay. Can I bring my puzzle? Show Neal?"

"Sure." She hoped he wouldn't be too disappointed if Neal wasn't there. "Let's put the pieces in your backpack so we don't drop any."

Anne bent down to retrieve the puzzle.

"Ian do it."

Holding the backpack open, she waited patiently while he dropped the pieces in one by one. A knock sounded at the door. She picked up Ian and went to answer it.

"Mommy said I could come over and see if you needed any help. Opal is already in her car seat," Rose said with seven-year-old superiority.

"No, we're all set. If you can walk Ian across the yard, I'll get his seat out of my car." Until Rose had mentioned car seats, she hadn't even thought about Ian needing his. Being a single parent was hard. She couldn't imagine how Neal had managed Autumn. He'd been barely more than a kid himself.

"I can do that," Rose said.

Anne put Ian down. "Go with Rose. I'm going to get your seat."

Ian stuck his thumb in his mouth and didn't move. What would she do if he refused to go? The childcare book she'd been reading said toddlers liked routine. Her forgetting the meeting and having to make last-minute babysitting arrangements had certainly upset the little bit of a routine they'd been able to establish.

Rose took Ian's other hand. "Come on. Grandma Mary said we could bake cookies with her."

"Cookies? Grandma's Ria bakes cookies for Ian."

Rose shot her funny look.

"Ian's grandmother in Boston. Maria is her housekeeper."

"Oh," Rose said, still looking confused. She tugged on Ian's hand and he trotted across the lawn with her. Anne followed with the car seat.

"I'll take that." Jamie strapped Ian's seat in the back between Opal's and Rose's. "In, guys," she said.

Anne held Ian close as she lifted him into his seat. "I'll be back soon. Have fun with the girls."

"Here's his backpack." She handed it to Jamie, who stashed it behind the seat, snapped Ian's car seat buckle and checked Rose's belt.

Anne stood behind her marveling at how efficiently Jamie had everyone in and ready to go. "You make it look so easy."

"What?" Jamie stepped back from the SUV and closed the door.

"Everything." Anne waved her hand at the three kids in the vehicle.

Jamie shrugged. "It gets easier with practice. And much easier with two parents."

The passenger-side window rolled down. "Mom," Myles said, "I told Tanner I'd be there by now."

"Tanner's dad is helping them with their science

project. I can't wait until John gets back. Eight more months and counting."

Anne's heart went out to Jamie, managing her family on her own. But it wouldn't be forever, not like… Anne halted her thought. She had no cause to be feeling sorry for herself. She was so lucky to have Ian and given time she'd get the hang of juggling work and parenthood.

"Should I bring Ian back with me or do you want to pick him up at the Hazards' after your meeting?"

"I'll pick him up. My meeting shouldn't last long."

Jamie walked around the front of the SUV to the driver's side. "And you might run into Neal if you do," she shot over the hood before climbing in and slamming the door.

Anne refused to dignify Jamie's tease with an answer because she might give away that she was thinking exactly the same thing.

"About time you got here," Emily said as Jamie herded Rose, Opal and Ian into the Hazards' home.

"I had to wait for Anne to get Ian's things together and drop Myles off at Tanner's house to work on his science project. Anne had an important meeting that she'd forgotten about and needed someone to watch Ian. I told her your mother wouldn't mind."

"I'm sure she wouldn't if she were here. She and

Dad drove Mrs. Donnelly to her cardiac appointment in Saranac. I guess her doctor didn't like something he saw and sent them up to a specialist in Plattsburgh."

"I guess that means no choir practice."

Emily shook her head. "I texted Autumn, but she's working at the nursing home this evening."

Behind Jamie, the outside door clicked open. "Hi, what's up?"

"Neal. Perfect."

"Yes, I am." He grinned. "But I never thought I'd get you to admit it, little sister."

"Here, take the baby. Mom was supposed to babysit for us so we could go to the special choir practice, but she got delayed."

Emily thrust Isabelle into his arms, grabbed her coat from the back of one of the kitchen chairs and she and Jamie were out the door before he could get a word out.

Isabelle patted his cheek and he rubbed noses with her. "How's my best girl?"

She gave him a drooly grin.

"Let's go see what I'm in for here." Neal carried her through the doorway into the dining room.

"Neal!" Opal squealed. "Where's Grandma Mary?"

"She had to do something and isn't home yet."

"So you're going to watch us?" Opal said, all smiles. "We brought Ian with us."

Neal followed her finger pointing under the

dining room table. There sat Ian surrounded by wooden puzzle pieces.

"Ne-al!" The little boy glanced upward at Opal. His little lips worked. "Neal." He corrected himself.

Neal's chest expanded with pride at the child's effort. "Hey, buddy. Want to come out and help me with Isabelle?"

"Puzzle," Ian said, patting his completed picture.

"It's a fire truck," Opal said with a touch of disgust. "I have a Dora the Explorer puzzle that has a lot more pieces."

Neal looked from Opal to her sister, who was seated at the table, to his niece in his arms. "We're outnumbered, buddy. We have to stick together. Bring your puzzle up here on the table and show me how you put it together."

"Stick to Neal."

More like Neal's stuck on Ian, Neal thought as he watched without the least bit of impatience as Ian crawled back and forth from under the table and placed his puzzle pieces on the table one by one. *And on Ian's Aunt Annie, if the truth be told.*

"Got them all?"

"One, two, three, seven, five." Ian touched the pieces.

"I'll count them for you," Opal said and counted the ten pieces. "They're all there," she said with authority.

"All there," Ian echoed.

"Hop up on a chair and we'll get to work," Neal said. The little boy scrambled up.

"Can you help me?" Rose asked from the chair on his other side. "We have to make sentences with our spelling words and I don't know how to spell *deployed*."

"D-e-p-l-o-y-e-d."

The little girl carefully wrote each letter on her worksheet.

"What's your sentence?"

"My daddy's unit is deployed. The spelling word is *unit*."

"Good sentence."

"Puzzle." Ian patted the table.

Not to be left out, Opal wedged herself between him and Rose and pushed a DVD in front of him. "I have a movie, *The Lion King*."

"Mommy said we're not supposed to watch the movie until I finish my homework." Rose pulled a coloring book and crayons out of the backpack next to her on table and pushed them toward Opal. "Here's your coloring stuff. I have three more words to do."

Opal flipped her coloring book open on Rose's paper and Neal's hand.

"Opal! I have to do my homework."

Neal lifted the book and placed it on the table across from him. "Opal, you can color on the other side of the table."

The little girl stuck out her lower lip and Ian patted the table again.

"Puzzle."

"If you sit on the other side of the table, Opal, you'll be able to show me your pictures better."

"Okay." She curled her fingers around the box and crayons, ducked under the table, and appeared on the other side.

Ian clapped, climbed off the chair and disappeared under the table. He popped up on the other side, grinned and crawled back to Neal.

He grabbed the toddler and lifted him to his lap. "Whoa. I thought we were going to do your puzzle."

Opal lifted her coloring book. "Look, Neal." She held up a hastily colored giraffe.

"How do you spell *tank?*" Rose asked.

"Puzzle," Ian said.

He was too old for this. Wooden puzzles, coloring books and second-grade homework were all things from his distant past, at least thirteen years distant. Neal looked around the table. Who was he kidding? He was enjoying himself far more than he would be reading his Western civilization assignment.

"Neal," Rose asked again, "how do you spell *tank?*"

"*T-a-n-k*. Are all of your sentences about your daddy?"

Rose nodded as she wrote the word. "I miss him."

"Me, too," Opal said.

Ian pushed his puzzle away. "Ian's daddy is gone."

"Is he in the army, too? Is that why you're living with Anne? Our daddy is coming home in the summer."

Neal tensed. Hadn't Jamie told the kids?

"No," Ian said, his wide eyes bright. "Mommy, Daddy gone."

"Opal, don't you remember what Mommy said?"

Opal's eyes went round and her mouth formed a perfect *O*. "Oh, yeah." She turned to Ian. "Neal told us that while our daddy is gone he could be our sub…sub…"

"Substitute," Rose filled in.

"Substitute daddy. Maybe he could be yours, too." She looked expectantly at Neal.

His heart stopped with the wanting. Wasn't that what he'd told himself he could do? Help Anne with Ian with no strings attached, like he helped Jamie.

Ian sniffled. Except there were strings, lots of strings, wrapped tightly around his heart tying him to Ian and Anne.

Anne couldn't believe how long the meeting had lasted. It was way past Ian's bedtime. Fortunately, she had late classes tomorrow morning. But what would Mary Hazard think? Jamie had probably picked her kids up an hour ago.

The only lights Anne saw on at the Hazards' as she approached were in the front, so she parked her car on the side of the road and went to the front door. Mary opened the door on the first knock.

Mary held her index finger to her lips as she let her in. "Shh." Mary motioned to the recliner where Neal sat snoozing with a sleeping Ian and a book on his lap. Anne's heart flip-flopped. They looked so natural together.

"Ted and I got home a few minutes ago and found them like that. They must have worn themselves out," she said, as if it were perfectly normal to come home to Ian being at her house.

"I had to go to a planning board meeting. I'd forgotten," Anne stammered, "and didn't have a babysitter. Jamie said you wouldn't mind since you were watching her kids and Isabelle anyway."

Mary nodded at her son. "I don't think Neal minded at all."

Anne didn't want to admit, even to herself, how much she'd like to hear those words from Neal.

Mary walked over and shook Neal's shoulder.

He opened his eyes. "Mom. I must have dozed off. Anne." He smiled sheepishly as he noticed her behind his mother. "We were reading *The Littlest Angel*. It was in a box of Autumn's books I have."

"We have it at home." Anne paused at how easily *home* rolled off her lips. "My grandmother gave it to me when I was little."

"I'll leave you guys alone."

Neal's gaze caught Anne's and when she broke the contact Mary had left.

Neal pushed the recliner upright and Ian stirred but didn't wake. "His snowsuit and stuff are here." He pointed to the floor beside him.

"I put him in the pj's you'd packed." Neal snuggled the warm form in his blanket sleeper.

Anne picked up Ian's backpack and slung it over her shoulder. "I'm sorry I'm so late. I was at a planning board meeting about the birthing center. Our attorney said the board approval was just a formality, which it was. What I didn't know is that we'd be the last item on the agenda."

"No problem. I was here, and Rose and Opal helped entertain him. Hand me his snowsuit. He's so sound asleep that I think we can get it on without waking him."

Anne lifted the navy blue suit from the floor and unzipped the front zippers. She leaned over to slip the legs over Ian's pajama-clad feet. Warmth and the smell of baby and something more masculine, much more masculine, assailed Anne, causing her to pause in her task.

"Need a hand?" Neal asked.

"No, I've got it. Can you lift him so I can get his arms in?" she contradicted herself.

Ian squirmed as she pulled the hood on his head and zipped up the snowsuit.

"Shh," she and Neal soothed in harmony.

He quieted and they grinned at each other.

Anne stood and Neal handed Ian to her. "We'd better get going."

Neal pushed out of the recliner to walk them to the door. "What are you doing for Thanksgiving?" he blurted. "I…we'd…Mom would like you to join us." He stumbled over his words, making her heart skip a beat.

"Thanks. But Margaret is planning to come and spend the weekend with us." Anne shut out the disappointment that engulfed her as she declined his invitation.

"I'm sure Mom would love for Margaret to come, too. What's one more at Thanksgiving?"

"Then we'd love to come," Anne said, despite the distinct feeling she had that Mary Hazard knew nothing about Neal's invitation. Or maybe especially because of that feeling.

Chapter Sixteen

Neal bounded out of the house in his shirtsleeves seemingly oblivious to the cold, gray Thanksgiving Day weather. "Let me give you a hand."

"Thanks," Anne said as she opened the car trunk. "We brought Margaret's walker for the day. She thought it would be easier than her wheelchair."

Neal lifted the walker from the trunk and unfolded it next to the passenger side of the car before he opened the door for Margaret.

"Good to see you again, Neal."

"Same here. Watch your step. The driveway is a little uneven." He helped her from the car.

"Neal," Ian called from the backseat. "We bring pie."

Anne opened the back door. "I asked your mom. It's pecan. Margaret's recipe." Why was she babbling? When she'd called Mary to see if she could bring anything, Neal's mother had said she could use another pie. She didn't need to explain herself.

"It was an act of self-defense."

"Pardon?" She unsnapped Ian's seat harness and he scrambled out of the car.

"Having you bring dessert, so Emily wouldn't. Last year she made something. We're still not sure what it was, and not because the rest of us haven't discussed it thoroughly."

Anne laughed. "I'm not sure I'm any better of a baker than your sister, but I had an expert to direct me."

Margaret accepted Neal's assistance to start toward the house. "She's being modest. All I provided was the recipe. It was my mother's. I remembered how much Anne liked it when she used to come home from college with Reenie to spend the holidays with us."

Remembering the good times she'd had with Reenie at her parent's house put a slight pall on Anne's holiday spirits. She covered it by grasping Ian's hand. "Let's go in. We can see baby Isabelle. He's been talking about her nonstop since the other night when you watched them."

Before Neal turned to walk Margaret to the house, a slow smile spread across his face that sent a tingle to her toes. The way he gently supported the older woman's elbow spoke to Anne of his strength, both inner and outer.

"Pie," Ian said, and pointed at the covered dish on the car floor.

"Right. We can't forget the pie." She released his hand and lifted the dessert from the floor.

Ian took off across the driveway and yard toward Neal and Margaret.

"Ian!" Anne shouted. "Stop and wait for me." She quickly caught up with him. "You know you're supposed to hold my hand. What if a car came up the driveway?"

"Neal," the toddler said as if that explained everything.

"He's fine," Margaret said.

Anne knew Margaret meant well, but Ian needed to mind her. She shuddered. He could have run into the road.

"Aunt Annie's right," Neal said with an apologetic nod to Margaret. "You need to hold her hand."

Anne warmed at Neal's support. It was so different than her parents had been with her. They'd seemed to work at undermining each other's authority.

Ian stuck his bottom lip out and looked at his grandmother.

Anne tensed. A disagreement with Margaret wasn't how she'd envisioned starting Thanksgiving dinner.

"You have to listen to Aunt Annie and Neal just like you listened to Mommy and Daddy. Understand?"

Anne's tension doubled. What was Margaret

doing? Ian was already upset. Margaret was about the last person she'd expect to be purposefully hurtful. Then again, her parents could put up a good front, too, when they wanted and to people who didn't know them well, they probably seemed like good parents.

Ian's lip slowly retreated and he nodded. "Listen to Nee Nee and—" he grinned "—Daddy Neal."

Anne dropped her gaze to the stone walkway as heat rose to her cheeks.

"That's Grandma's big boy," Margaret said with a chuckle.

When Anne lifted her gaze to continue into the house, Neal was looking at her with a bemused expression on his handsome face.

The door to the house opened. "Are you coming in or moving the party outside?" Ted Hazard asked.

Ian tugged on Neal's pant leg. "Who's that?"

"That's *my* dad," Neal said.

Neal lifted Ian to the first step. "Us guys are going to help your grandma up the stairs."

Margaret released her walker and leaned on Neal's arm. He handed to walker to his dad.

"Take Grandma's other arm."

Margaret fought to keep a straight face as Ian solemnly did as told.

"Wait," Neal said. "Maybe we should let Aunt Annie help. We don't want her to feel left out."

"Nee Nee help, too."

Ted held the door open and Neal, Anne and Ian guided Margaret into the house.

"I'm Ted Hazard," he said as he closed the door behind them.

"Margaret Cabot."

"Come in and sit down. Mary and Emily are in the kitchen. They have everything under control there. This is my son-in-law, Drew, and granddaughter, Isabelle."

Neal hung back while his father made the introductions.

Ted and Anne helped Margaret settle on the couch.

"I'll take the pie into the kitchen," Anne said. "Ian, stay with Grandma and play with your toys."

She let the backpack that was slung over her shoulder drop to the floor. "That is, if you don't mind."

"Mind time with my favorite grandson? Not a chance."

"I know what you mean," Ted said as he scooped up Isabelle and eased into the recliner.

Ian pulled a fire truck from his pack and ran it up Ted's leg toward Isabelle. "Vroom, vroom." He smiled shyly when the man looked at him and scooted back to his grandmother.

"Our oldest is nineteen." Ted looked down at Isabelle and Ian. "We've been waiting a while for some more."

Neal coughed and Anne escaped to the kitchen, feeling his eyes on her until she was out of sight.

Emily poked her head in the doorway. "Mom is out of olive oil for the salad. Can you walk down to the lodge and get ours?"

"Sure." Drew rolled from the couch to his feet. "Need anything else?"

"No, that should do it. Dad, you okay with Izzie? I could take her."

"We'll be fine." Ted chucked the infant under the chin and she laughed.

"Okay, then. I'll get back to peeling potatoes."

"Neal, want to walk down with me?"

"Yeah." He could use a break from Dad's not-at-all-subtle comments about grandchildren.

Neal and Drew shrugged on their jackets. The wind had picked up since Anne and Ian had arrived, making the seasonal high-thirties temperature feel colder. Neal tucked his hands in his pockets and ducked his head.

"I'm glad you took my advice." Drew pulled leather gloves from his pockets.

Neal frowned. "Advice? What advice?"

"Back when Anne first came to Bible study. I said not to fight it. You'd be ahead of the game."

Neal wanted to disagree, but he couldn't. He *had* invited Anne to Thanksgiving dinner with his folks. But he wasn't going to let his brother-in-law take credit for his change of heart toward Anne and Ian. He'd had a soft spot for each of them since they'd arrived in Paradox Lake.

"What makes you think you had anything to do with it?"

"You've got me there. Nothing anyone said had any effect on me until I figured out myself that I was in love with Emily."

"I'm not."

Drew gave him a pointed look.

"Okay, I probably am."

"Probably?" Drew snickered.

"Okay. You're right. I'm falling for Anne. Does that make you feel better?" Neal's voice echoed through the forest surrounding the Sonrise Camp lodge at a volume he feared would carry down to his folks' house.

"Yep. It's a good place to be. Glad to see you finally made it. Want to come in?" Drew started up the steps to the lodge.

"No, I'll wait out here." Pacing in the bitter wind might take some heat out of the realization that he wanted to try to make a life with Anne and Ian.

"Dinner's ready." Mary Hazard ushered everyone into the dining room.

Anne worked to keep the smile from her face when Mary seated her next to Neal. First Ted with his grandchildren comment. Now Mary. She glimpsed at Neal's profile. Maybe it was time to give in to the prodding and chance going where her heart would take her. If only she had a grasp on Neal's feelings for her and Ian.

At the head of the table, Ted waited for everyone to sit. "Everything looks—" he breathed in "—and smells so good. I won't take too long, but some thanks are due."

Neal took her hand and she took Margaret's, who took Ian's. A warm peace flowed around the table as they all bowed their heads.

"Lord, thank You for providing us with this abundance of food when so many around the world will go hungry today. Thank You for the company of good friends, Anne and Margaret and little Ian, and for my family here. We wish Autumn was with us, but she's doing Your work today helping others. And thank You for looking over us all, bringing Emily home and giving Drew the backing to continue Sonrise Camp, Neal opportunities and direction as he moves into a new phase in his life, and Mary and me the blessing of Isabelle and freedom from want as we head toward retirement. Amen."

He lifted his fork. "Now, let's enjoy this wonderful meal Mary and Emily and Anne prepared for us."

Anne opened her mouth to protest that she hadn't done much to contribute to the bounty in front of them, but Neal's quick squeeze of her hand stopped her. She let herself take pleasure in being included with the Hazard women.

During dinner, Anne joined in the family chatter and camaraderie with none of the uneasiness she'd felt at the impromptu barbeque at Emily and Drew's earlier in the fall. She let her gaze drift from Ian to Margaret and around the table ending with Neal, who held it a moment before returning to his dinner. Joy bubbled up inside her. *This was what family was all about.*

After they'd passed all of the dishes around at least twice, Mary asked if everyone wanted pie and coffee now or later.

Ted patted his stomach. "Later sounds good to me, but I'll take some coffee."

"Just coffee here, too," Emily said.

Everyone else nodded in agreement.

"Anne, would you help me?"

"Sure," she answered, confused as to what help Mary would need. Unless it was an excuse to speak to her alone for some reason. Before Anne could stop it her mind raced back over her dinner conversation. Coming up with nothing Mary could take as improper, Anne shook off the silly notion that she was in for a reprimand for some indiscretion.

"I wanted to thank you for coming. I know it means a lot to Neal, even if he hasn't let you in on that information."

The heat of the kitchen made Anne's face warm.

"He's never asked a woman to a family dinner before, not since Autumn's mother, and he was still a kid then."

Anne's heartbeat ticked up. She didn't know how to respond.

Mary unplugged the silver percolator. "Let's get the coffee out before the guys all fall asleep at the table. The creamers are in the refrigerator. I have milk and half-and-half."

Anne found them and followed Mary back to the dining room.

"Neal," she heard Margaret say as they passed through the doorway. "Anne told me you're interested in solar energy."

She'd done more than tell Margaret about Neal's interest. She'd told her all about the plans Neal had drawn up for the birthing center and how he'd impressed the representatives from GoSolar and the other companies vying for the project. She'd also confided in her about the Green Spaces scholarship.

"My neighbors recently had a system installed by GoSolar and they can't say enough good things about the system or the company."

A grin spread across Neal's face. "Small world. I just signed a contract to work with GoSolar doing the final electrical hookups for their photovoltaic systems."

"So, you made a decision," Ted said.

"But you don't have to," Anne blurted. She'd thought about telling Neal about the scholarship a dinner so his family could celebrate with him, bu not exactly like this.

Everyone stared at her.

"You don't have to take on the extra work."

They continued to stare.

Milk, or was it half-and-half, spilled over the sid of one of the creamers and dribbled down her hand to the floor. What was wrong with her?

She placed the creamers on the table and put he most engaging business smile on her face. "Wha I meant to say is that I have an announcement."

The stares turned to curious looks.

"For Neal in particular."

His eyes lit. She couldn't wait to see his expres sion when he heard her next words.

"You don't have to take on the extra work. I know it's probably been a struggle juggling your busines and school and paying for your and Autumn's tu ition and other expenses."

The light in his eyes dimmed. Had she embar rassed him by mentioning money? Men could be so sensitive about providing for their families.

"Green Spaces is going to award you one of it annual scholarships. Starting next semester, we'l pay your tuition and books, plus a stipend for liv ing expenses. And, once you graduate from NCC and transfer to RPI, the scholarship amount wil increase to cover tuition and books there, along with living expenses."

"What if I want to work for GoSolar? What if I'm not planning on going to RPI or even finishing at NCCC?" His voice had an edge that sliced right through her.

"I…" She pulled herself together. "This is a real opportunity. Thousands of students compete for these scholarships every year."

"Because they want them."

"And you don't," she countered in disbelief.

Ted cleared his throat. "Neal, maybe you and Anne would like to take your conversation somewhere more private."

Anne cringed with memories of her father and, at times, her husband, Michael, reminding her of how she should comport herself in front of company and clients.

"Let's take a walk."

The open architecture of the Hazard's home made outdoors or Neal's apartment over the garage the only choices for any privacy.

"After you." Neal rose and pulled her chair out so she could stand.

The forceful way he shoved the chair back under the table conveyed his anger louder than words. All because she wanted to help him? While he was undeniably masculine, he'd never struck her as too macho to accept help.

"You'll want gloves and a hat or scarf if you have one," he said as he handed Anne her coat from the front closet. "You can use one of Emily's old ones if you don't." He reached for his cap and gloves from the closet shelf.

Anne put her coat on in silence and pulled her earmuffs and gloves from her pockets. She wrapped her scarf around the collar of the coat and threw the one end over her shoulder. Neal held the outside door open for her.

She stopped at the bottom of the steps. "I don't see why you're so angry."

"We'd better walk if we want to stay warm." Neal strode out to the road. Despite his longer stride, she matched him step for step.

"Working and going to school full-time can't be easy."

He shrugged. "People do it."

She refused to rise to his bait. "With the scholarship, you wouldn't have to take on the extra work with GoSolar. You wouldn't even have to work at all."

He glared at her.

"Unless you wanted to. If you transfer to RPI at the end of this school year you should be able to finish your environmental engineering degree in three, three and a half more years."

A muscle worked in his jaw but he didn't say anything.

"Obviously, Troy is too far to commute to. But

it's not too far to come home weekends to see Autumn and your family." She breathed deeply and the sharp cold air stung her lungs. "And Ian and me." There. She'd said aloud what had been smoldering between them.

He raised an eyebrow.

Her heart raced. "You'd have a place at Green Spaces when you finish. We hire a lot of our scholarship students."

He stopped walking and her throat tightened.

"You could have an office in Ticonderoga."

"Are you done?"

"Yes."

"I'm not a subsidiary of Green Spaces."

What was he talking about?

"You can't develop a business plan for my life and just expect to carry it out, business as usual."

"That's not—"

"Isn't it?"

She shook her head. It wasn't.

Neal turned to her and placed his hands gently on her upper arms. She shivered, but not from the cold.

"We should turn back."

He placed his arm around her shoulder and she wanted to pretend she'd never brought up the scholarship, that they weren't having this conversation.

"I didn't agree to work with GoSolar just for the money." His voice was low and soft now. "I thought and prayed about it long and hard. It's what I want to do. Engineering was what I thought I wanted to do twenty years ago. That was then. This is now. I'm a different person. We're both different people. I'm going to finish out the semester at NCCC. Then I'm done."

"You're quitting?" She bit her tongue. "I mean, you could finish your environmental studies degree at NCCC part-time. Then—"

His eyes clouded and his face went slack. "You're hearing me but not listening. Does my not having a degree matter so much?"

She wanted to say no but on some level it seemed it did.

Neal's cell phone rang.

"Go ahead," she said, glad for the reprieve.

He dropped his arm from her shoulders. "It's the house," he said before answering.

Anne swallowed. Was something wrong with Ian? Surely, Mary and Margaret could handle anything that might be.

"We'll be right there."

"Ian?"

"What?" His expression softened. "No, Autumn called. The power went out at the nursing home. They're running the generator to keep the heat going. She wants me to come see if I can do anything. Fortunately, about half of the residents are with family for the holiday."

"You're going to go?"

His eyes narrowed. "Of course I'm going to go. It's not like I have some underling I can send."

"I didn't mean it like that. I meant… Never mind." She didn't know what she meant. "You were right at Margaret's when you said I didn't know you at all. And you don't know me."

And she'd already spent eleven years in a marriage where her husband didn't really know her or care to.

He bent and pressed his lips to hers so softly and quickly she wasn't sure it had happened until she felt his warm breath on her frosty cheek.

"I'm sorry I'm not the guy you want me to be." He left her at the steps and strode to his truck.

An arrow of pain struck her heart, leaving a dull ache. It wasn't like he was breaking off their relationship. They didn't really *have* a relationship. Anne touched her cheek with her cold gloved fingers. She didn't need Neal. She and Ian were doing fine with just the two of them and they could continue to do just fine. Couldn't they?

Chapter Seventeen

Ian coughed himself awake and Anne picked him up from the couch where she'd tucked him in a half hour ago with his *Muppets* DVD playing on the TV. He was still warm. Maybe even warmer than when she'd laid him down. She'd checked the health handbook from her insurance provider and given him children's Tylenol like the nurse she'd talked to on the help line had told her. *His temperature should be coming down.*

When the day care teacher had called Anne Friday afternoon to ask her to pick up Ian early, the teacher had assured her it was probably a bug that had been going around school. The other kids had been fine in a day or two. But it was five o'clock Sunday and Ian wasn't anywhere near fine. Why hadn't she taken him to the pediatrician yesterday during the Saturday-morning emergency office hours?

"Nee Nee." He raised his arms to her and coughs racked his little body.

She lifted him onto her lap. Not only was he hot, but he was also limp and his eyes were glassy. Fear paralyzed her.

"I hurt," Ian whimpered.

Anne rubbed his back and comforted him, looking out the living room window at Jamie's dark house. Jamie would know what to do. But Jamie wasn't home yet from her folks' in Buffalo.

Ian wheezed into another coughing fit and started crying, which only aggravated the coughing.

A flash of headlights caught her eye as a vehicle turned into Jamie's driveway. Anne rose, lifting Ian to her shoulder. *Yes, finally.* But the lights didn't look right for Jamie's van. The vehicle stopped a short way into the drive and backed out. Her heart sank. It was only someone turning around.

Anne paced the living room, which seemed to soothe Ian. She hadn't felt this helpless since, since she'd been a child herself.

Mary. Neal's mother. She could call her. Anne carried Ian into the kitchen and lifted the phone receiver from the wall. She dialed the Hazards' number. Her chest tightened as the phone rang and rang. What if Neal answered?

Ian coughed and rubbed his face against her. She was being silly. So, what if Neal did answer?

He'd probably know what to do as well as his mother would.

"Hello," Mary Hazard said.

"Mrs. Hazard, Mary. It's Anne Howard."

"Anne, what's wrong?"

How did Mary know something was wrong? Most likely from her near-hysterical voice. She needed to calm herself.

"It's Ian. He's running a temperature. I've done everything the health handbook and the helpline nurse I talked with said to do, and I can't get it down." She took a gulp of air. "I've been waiting for Jamie and the kids to get back from visiting her parents. I'm concerned. I thought you'd know something I could do."

"I'll be right over."

"You don't… Thank you. I really appreciate this."

"Have you been giving him liquids?"

"He didn't want his milk."

"Try some cool water or watered-down apple juice. I'll see you in a few minutes."

"Thanks again."

Anne fixed Ian a sippy cup of juice and walked him back to the living room. She sank into the chair, buried her face in his carrot curls and prayed.

"Please Lord. I tried to do everything I was supposed to. Please help Ian feel better."

It came out stilted, but lightened her worry a bit just the same.

To Anne, the fifteen minutes it took Mary to drive to her house seemed to take an hour. The sound of the car pulling in had her on her feet and at the door before Mary was out of the car.

Anne swung the door open and the older woman rushed in.

"Let me see that baby," Mary said in a lilting voice. She took Ian from Anne's arms. "You don't feel good, do you?"

Ian made a halfhearted attempt to pull away from Mary and lift his arms to Anne. Her throat clogged.

"He's really warm. What was his temperature last time you took it?"

A sense of inadequacy that Anne hadn't experienced in years filled her. "It was one hundred two before I got him down to sleep about an hour ago." She should have taken it again when he'd woken.

"We should check again."

Mary sat with Ian and Anne handed her the thermometer from the end table.

A minute later, Mary handed it back. "My glasses are in my purse."

Anne checked the thermometer and swallowed the clog that had stuck in her throat. "One hundred and four. I gave him the Tylenol," she said as much to herself as to Mary. "It should have gone down."

"Who's your doctor?"

Anne gave Mary the name of a practice in Ticonderoga.

"We use them, too. Call their service and tell them we're taking Ian to the Saranac Lake hospital." Mary gave Ian back to Anne. "I'll move Ian's car seat into my car. I just filled the tank. Is the garage locked?"

Anne nodded yes and then no, conserving her words for the call to the doctor's service. She kissed Ian's warm forehead. Why hadn't she gone with her first inclination and taken him to the doctor's yesterday morning instead of following the protocol in the health handbook and waiting to make sure it wasn't an "unnecessary visit," as the book had discussed?

After she finished the call, Anne bundled Ian in his snowsuit.

Mary came back in from outside. "All set. I'll take him so you can put your coat on."

This time, Ian went to Neal's mother with no protest. He didn't seem to have the energy.

Anne opened the door for Mary and Ian. A cutting wind fought to yank the handle from her grasp and slam the door against the house. She held fast and forced it shut behind Mary.

Head down against the wind, Mary tucked Ian's face under the lapel of her coat and led the way to her car.

"I'm going to ride in the back with Ian." Anne opened the back door of the car.

"Of course." Mary handed her Ian and she strapped him in his seat before walking around to the other side of the car.

Within the first ten miles of the fifty-mile drive to the hospital, Ian fell into a fitful sleep.

Anne adjusted his wool cap to cover his ears better, even though the car was plenty warm. "You're a godsend. I didn't know what to do."

"I'll bet that's a situation you don't often find yourself in."

Anne grasped the edge of Ian's seat. Criticism wasn't something she'd expected from Mary.

"You've always had such an air of confidence, even when you were a teen."

A hard-earned confidence that motherhood was taking a toll on.

"And that same methodical way of thinking that Neal has. But, tell me if I'm wrong, it's different when it's your child, isn't it? Decisions aren't as clear-cut."

"Exactly," Anne said with relief. Maybe she wasn't as inept as she was beginning to feel. "I thought I should take Ian to the doctor yesterday, but the health handbook and the information I read online said I should wait a while longer to see if his temperature went down."

"Did you pray on it?"

Anne clenched her jaw. "I prayed hard for Ian." She didn't want to get into her track record on getting any personal direction from prayer.

"When Neal was a new father, my mother cross-stitched him a verse that had always been dear to her heart, Proverbs 3:5–6. 'Trust in the Lord with all your heart and lean not on your own understanding; in all your ways acknowledge Him and He will make your paths straight.'"

So, that's where he got it from. But because it worked for him, didn't mean it worked for everyone. If the Lord had told her what to do today, she wouldn't have had to call Mary. Or had He told her to call Mary? She rubbed her temples. She didn't have the patience to think about theology now. She just wanted Ian well.

The hospital came in sight and saved her from having to respond to Mary.

"Take Ian in," Mary said as she pulled up to the emergency room entrance. "I'll park the car and meet you inside."

Anne held the half-asleep Ian on her hip while she pulled open the glass door to the emergency room. It was blessedly empty. She explained everything to an intake person behind a glass window.

"Yes, your doctor called." The woman buzzed open a door and had Anne sit in a chair next to her desk.

"Please fill out this short form."

Anne rearranged Ian on her lap so she could write down the information.

"And I'll need to make a copy of your insurance card, if you have it with you."

Anne dug in her wallet for the card, spilling the contents on the desk when it slipped out of her hand. "Here." She picked up the insurance card and shoved it at the woman. "Couldn't we do this later?" she asked in a surprising calm and even voice.

The woman ran the card through a desktop scanner. "You're set now. Follow me." She led them back to a curtained cubical and put up the side rails of the stretcher that took up most of the room. "A nurse will be with you shortly."

Anne placed Ian on the stretcher and removed his snowsuit before taking off her coat and placing it on the chair crammed in next to the side curtain.

"They're in E4," she heard the intake person say. Anne looked at the number on the back wall over the stretcher. *E4. That must be Mary.*

The curtain moved. "How is he?" The unexpected deep voice made her heart leap.

"Neal. What are you doing here?" she blurted.

He waved her off. "Later. Has the doctor seen him?"

"No, we just got back here. Insurance stuff. A nurse is supposed to be coming."

Ian coughed and wheezed as if he were struggling for breath.

"I'll see where that nurse is." Neal was gone as quickly as he'd appeared.

Anne stroked Ian's curls, glad for Neal and his taking charge. She didn't care about the *whys* and the *wherefores*. She was physically tired, and tired of being in charge.

"Neal?" Ian opened his eyes and looked around the cubicle.

"He'll be right back, baby."

Ian closed his eyes again.

The other day when she and Neal had argued, she'd been determined that she and Ian were fine, just the two of them. But she'd been wrong, like she was wrong to try and mold Neal into what she thought he wanted to be, wrong about him not knowing her—he might know her better than she did—and wrong not to have taken Ian to the doctor's yesterday.

She gazed at Ian's still, flushed little face and folded her hands. "Lord," she said in an angry whisper, "is this the way you're speaking to me, telling me to right my wrongs? Through a helpless little boy?" She knew her accusation wasn't right, but the words poured out. "Stop. I get it. Make him well. Make us all well."

Her mind raced trying to come up with some direction.

Think with your heart and not with your head.

Was that something Mary had said on the drive to the hospital? Anne couldn't remember, but it was worth a try.

Two steps outside the cubicle, Neal almost walked into the nurse and a doctor.

"Mr. McCabe?" the nurse asked.

Neal's heart sank and his aggravation grew. They weren't coming to see Ian.

"Are you with Ian McCabe?"

McCabe. Neal hadn't known the boy's last name. There were so many things he didn't know or thought he knew but didn't.

"I'm a friend of his…his aunt's."

The nurse narrowed her eyes and pulled the curtain aside to reveal Anne bent over, her lips pressed to Ian's forehead. She jerked back, her face pale.

Neal's throat clogged. He brushed past the doctor and nurse and placed his arm around her shoulder. What he wanted was to take her in his arms and reassure her that everything would be all right, that he'd keep her and Ian safe forever. But that wasn't something he had the power to promise. She leaned against him as if grateful for the support. A sense of rightness filled him. He loved her and Ian. He had for a while. He just hadn't wanted to admit it to himself until his conversation with Drew on Thanksgiving. And angry as he'd been with Anne after dinner, their argument hadn't done anything to diminish the strength of that love.

"I'm Dr. Carson," the pediatric resident introduced himself. "Kristen will take the baby's vitals while you tell me the problem."

"Anne Howard." She extended her hand for a handshake. "And this is…a family friend, Neal Hazard." She rushed into an explanation of Ian's condition.

"He does sound very wheezy." The doctor glanced at the notations the nurse had written on the chart on the foot of the bed. "I want to listen to his lungs. Kristen, sit him up."

"Nee Nee. Want Nee Nee." Ian started crying.

"That's me. Aunt Annie." She pulled away from Neal and soothed the toddler. "I'm right here. It's okay. The doctor is going to listen to you breathe so he can make you better."

She looked from Ian to the doctor, her eyes wide with a silent plea that tore at Neal's insides.

The doctor leaned down. "Hi, Ian, I'm Dr. Carson. I'm going to use my stethoscope to hear what's going on inside you and making you feel sick." He offered his scope to Ian and let him touch it before he pressed the diaphragm to his back.

Anne rubbed Ian's little fleece-encased leg in reassurance.

"Can you breathe in a deep breath?" Dr. Carson showed Ian. "Good boy. Now, I'm going to listen to you from the front." He moved the stethoscope to the boy's chest. "Another deep breath. Good job. You can lay back down on the pillow now."

Ian turned his head to Anne. She nodded and pulled the sheet up over him.

"I want to get X-rays of his lungs," Dr. Carson said. "Someone from transportation will be down shortly to take him over to X-ray."

Anne turned from the bed and Neal took her hand and squeezed. They were in this together.

"What's wrong?" she asked as the doctor reached for the cubical curtain.

"It may be pneumonia. The X-rays will tell. I'll be back to talk with you after the report. We'll probably admit him."

Anne gripped Neal's hand. "Okay. Thank you." She sank into the molded plastic chair next to the bed.

Neal rubbed his thumb against the top of her hand. "Pneumonia. Poor little guy."

"I should have—"

He released her hand and pressed his index finger to her lips. "You did fine. You got him here and they'll take care of him. Everything will be all right."

"Ian McCabe?" The transportation aide pulled the curtains back.

"Yes," Anne answered in a rusty voice.

The man checked his clipboard against the wristband the nurse had put on Ian and asked for his date of birth. He positioned a stretcher next to the bed and lifted Ian onto it.

Anne shot out of the chair to stand at the end of the bed next to the stretcher.

Ian made only a feeble protest as the aide gently strapped the belts over him.

"You can put his things in this bag." The aide handed Anne a plastic bag with a tag that matched Ian's wristband.

Neal took it from her and packed Ian's snowsuit, hat and mittens. He handed it back and the aide placed it on the bottom of the stretcher.

"Follow me." The aide pushed the stretcher out of the cubicle and emergency room with Anne right behind.

Neal gathered her and his coats and quickly caught up. As they walked in silence to the X-ray department, Neal prayed that the words he'd spoken to Anne in the emergency room had been the truth. Ian was so little. Autumn had had all of the usual childhood diseases and mishaps, but he'd never had to take her to the hospital. He gazed at Anne's pale profile. Ian *had* to be all right.

Neal paced behind her in Ian's hospital room in the children's unit. *Poor baby.* He looked so small against the stark white sheets of the hospital bed with the IV bag looming over him.

"Where's the doctor?" Neal stopped behind Anne's chair and dropped his hands to her shoulders.

She glanced up at the clock. They'd been in here seven minutes. It seemed like an hour. Before she could say anything to him, a nurse wheeled in a small table with some sort of device on it.

"I'm Tammy. I'll be Ian's nurse tonight. This is a nebulizer." She motioned to the device. "Dr. Carson prescribed it to help open Ian's airways."

"Then he has pneumonia," Neal said.

"The doctor will be in shortly to talk with you."

Neal squeezed her shoulders, an action Anne figured was as much to reassure himself as to reassure her. She didn't know how she'd ever be able to thank him enough for being here. He hadn't had to come or stay. She looked up over her shoulder at him and glimpsed a momentary expression of helplessness before he regained control of his features.

The floodgates of her heart opened. She loved him, and he cared for her on some level. She knew he did. She returned her gaze to Ian. Maybe they had a chance for something together after all, even if it were only friendship. She could live with that—for now.

The nurse unwrapped a face mask from the tubing attached to the nebulizer. She placed the mask over the sleeping child's nose and mouth and turned it on. The machine's whirring sound woke Ian and he pulled at the mask.

"Whoa, buddy. You need to leave that on." Neal strode over to the bed. "It's medicine to make you better."

Ian pawed at it again.

"You should see yourself. All the puffy white smoke you're making. You look like the dragon in your storybook."

Ian stopped pulling at the mask and raised his eyes to view the smoke drifting up.

"Aunt Annie, why don't you take a picture of Ian with your phone so he can see tomorrow after the medicine has made him feel all better?"

Anne blinked the moisture from her eyes and retrieved her phone from her coat pocket. "Is it okay?" she asked the nurse, remembering the many signs posted on the hospital walls saying to turn off cell phones.

"I won't tell if you don't."

Anne clicked a couple of photos of Ian, along with one of Neal leaning over and chucking Ian under the chin.

The nurse checked the settings on the nebulizer. "Like I said, the doctor will be in soon. If you're going to stay, the chair folds out to a cot and I can bring in another one from another room."

"We're going to stay," Neal said.

"I'll go get the chair." The nurse left.

"Ian has pneumonia. How could she think we wouldn't stay? He's hardly more than a baby."

Anne bit back a smile at Neal's indignation and the fact that he'd once thought worse of her.

After a fitful night punctuated by the nurse's periodic checks of Ian's vital signs, Anne woke to the hum of Neal's gentle snoring from the other side of Ian's bed, but no sound from Ian. Her heart stopped until she saw the rhythmic rise and fall of his chest. She stood and touched his forehead. It was cool.

"How is he?" Neal whispered, running his hand through his sleep-tousled hair.

"He feels much cooler."

"I'm so glad." Neal moved around the bed and took her in his arms. She leaned her head on his chest and listened to the thumping of his heart.

A knock at the door pulled them apart.

An older man with a round face and twinkling eyes smiled from the doorway. "I'm Dr. Klein. Looks like you already know my good news."

The doctor's voice woke Ian. He looked around and blinked in confusion until he saw Anne.

"Why don't you introduce me to this young man and I'll check him out to see if he's ready to go home."

The doctor finished his examination. "I'm going to release him to recuperate at home. The nurse will come in and go over my instructions with you. You'll need to schedule a follow-up with your doctor next week." He smiled down at Ian. "Ready to go home with Mom and Dad?"

Anne's muscles froze. Of course the doctor didn't know. She braced herself for Ian's and Neal's reactions.

Ian tilted his head and nodded. "Daddy Neal."

Her tension increased until a chuckle from Neal melted it.

"Daddy Neal. I like it."

"Sorry," Dr. Klein said. "I assumed. I hope I haven't caused a problem." He glanced over at Ian. "My office staff is always after me to be more careful about things like that."

"No problem," Neal said. "It's nothing we can't fix."

Was he talking about him and her? Anne gripped the bed rail to steady herself.

Dr. Klein left, but before she could say anything to Neal, an aide came in with Ian's breakfast, followed shortly by the nurse with Dr. Klein's instructions and the transportation aide with a wheelchair for Ian.

"I'll go down and bring the car around to the front door," Neal said.

Anne nodded and settled Ian in the chair.

"Like Gammy's," he said.

"Right," she said, her thoughts circling back to Neal's cryptic statement. For once, she'd been able to hold her tongue with him and not blurt out her questions. They should talk in private when Ian wasn't with them. He was such a smart inquisitive child. And her interpretation of Neal's words might simply be wishful thinking.

Neal backed his mother's car out of the parking space and pulled around the corner of the hospital. Mom and Dad had taken his truck and left the car for him and Anne to bring Ian home. His heart warmed. He liked the sound of that. He and Anne bringing Ian home. Neal knew now that he wanted Anne and Ian and everything being a family brought with it. And he prayed that he could convince Anne that she did, too.

He knew he was different than Anne's first husband and probably from any of the men she'd dated before or since. He believed in his heart that he was the right man for her.

Neal tapped the top of the steering wheel. He'd take things slow, woo her. Once Ian was better, he'd ask Autumn to babysit and take Anne to a movie in Schroon Lake, out to dinner locally a few times. He could invite her and Ian and Margaret to share Christmas with his folks and Emily and Drew. Then, for New Year's, he'd take her somewhere special, maybe down to Lake George for a fancy dinner at the Sagamore Resort. And tell her he loved her and wanted to make his life with her. Yep, that's what he'd do. Take things nice and slow.

He stopped the car in front of the hospital and hopped out. His pulse quickened when he saw Anne with Ian waiting for him behind the glass doors. He strode over and took Ian from her arms.

"Everybody ready?"

"More than ready," Anne said, clutching the doctor's instructions in her hand. The tinge of blue below her eyes spoke how hard the past few days had been on her.

"Come on." He squeezed her to his side with his free hand and helped her and Ian into the car.

Obviously feeling better, Ian chattered nonstop for about twenty minutes into the drive home and then dropped off to sleep in the middle of a sentence.

Neal looked over at Anne. "I'm okay if you want to rest, too."

She gave him a wan smile. "I'm afraid I'm too tired to sleep." She rubbed the bridge of her nose. "I can't tell you how much I appreciate everything you and your family have done for Ian and me."

He concentrated on navigating the winding road. "That's what fam—friends—are for."

"No. You didn't have to drive all the way to Saranac and stay with me until Ian was out of danger. Especially after Thanksgiving."

"I didn't do anything I wouldn't do for anyone I love." Neal clenched the steering wheel. He didn't say that aloud, did he?

"You love me?"

Anne's soft response confirmed his fear. So much for his plan to take things slow. He kept his eyes focused on the road. Might as well lay it all out. The worst that could happen is she could smash his heart to smithereens.

"Yes, I love you," he managed to say. "And I love Ian and I want to make a life with you."

"But you don't want kids. You've said that, several times."

He jerked his head to the right. It wasn't like Anne to throw his words back at him.

The corners of her mouth tipped up. "Better keep your eyes on the road."

He relaxed. She was teasing.

"And you don't want a husband who doesn't have a college degree."

"I never said that."

He swallowed. He might as well go for the goal. "Nor have you said you love me."

Neal watched her out of the corner of his eye. She raised her chin and closed her eyes as if thinking hard. Apprehension sucked all of the air out of the car.

"Yes," she finally said. "That's the plan. You love me. I love you."

All right! If he weren't driving, he'd grab Anne and kiss her senseless.

"Still planning, are you?" He couldn't resist teasing her back.

She bit her lip and nodded. "But now I'm planning with my heart."

Neal pressed the brake and turned onto an old dirt logging trail cut into the pines.

"What are you doing?" Her voice rose.

"Something I haven't done in a long time."

She cocked her head to the side.

"Parking in the woods with my best girl." He stopped the car, pulled Anne into his arms and kissed her, a kiss that promised a lifetime of love—and much, much more.

Epilogue

Eighteen months later

"Hello." Anne knocked and called through the screen door of the Sonrise Camp Lodge. She rubbed her lower back while she waited for a response. She'd thought a stroll down Hazard Cove Road from the log home she and Neal had built between his parents' house and the lodge would relieve the off and on ache she'd had since last night.

"Hi, come in." Emily opened the door wide for her very pregnant sister-in-law. "What's up?"

"With classes out for the semester, I'm bored. Ian's at preschool, and Neal's still out of town finishing that solar job south of Albany. So I thought I'd bake chocolate chip cookies for my guys when they get home. But I'm out of baking powder. Do you have any I could borrow?"

"Sure do. And how are the little Hazards?" Emily pointed at Anne's distended belly.

"Right now, they seem to be having a competi-tion to see who can kick me hardest in the back." Anne bent over and hugged herself. "They've moved the competition to the front."

Emily helped her to a chair. "How long have you been having contractions?"

"What?" Anne rubbed her belly. "These are Braxton-Hicks contractions, false labor. I've been having them for the past couple of weeks."

"How often?"

Anne hesitated. She didn't want to be in labor, not until Neal got back from Albany. She was hop-ing if she ignored the pain and kept busy, they'd go away like they had before.

"A couple, three times an hour."

"Since when?"

"Yesterday." She hadn't said anything to Neal when he'd called last night. She didn't want him rushing home for nothing.

"Call Kelly and tell her I'm bringing you to the birthing center."

"But I'm not due until next month."

"You're having twins. Call her."

"You know, you can be very bossy," Anne shot back, glad Emily had made the decision for her. She'd almost called her midwife, Kelly, last night and again earlier this morning. But she'd checked her pregnancy and childbirth guide and convinced herself it was false labor.

"So I've been told. I'll call Drew while you're calling Kelly. He took Isabelle with him to hang the trail markers for the first camp session next week. We can leave as soon as he gets back here to stay with Sam. Mom or Drew will pick Ian up from school."

Anne smiled. She loved being a part of the Hazard family and that her and Neal's twins would have a built-in playmate in their six-week-old cousin Sam.

"And get ahold of my big brother and tell him to get himself back here pronto. I know what it's like to be in labor and not have my husband beside me."

Drew and Isabelle trooped in as Anne hung up from calling Neal. When he hadn't picked up, she'd left a message. Then, she'd texted just in case, praying he hadn't left his phone in the truck.

"Let's go. We've still got to stop by your house for your hospital bag."

Anne plodded out behind Emily as if postponing her arrival at the birthing center would give Neal more time to retrieve her message and get back here.

Neal flew into the birthing center. How could he have left his phone in the truck? If he hadn't gone back to get his tester… He didn't want to think about it. When he'd called Drew, his brother-in-law said Anne and Emily had just left. He'd driven as fast as he dared.

"Dad. You made it. Come on. Anne sent me out to check again whether you'd arrived. I think she's been willing the babies to wait until you got here."

He smiled at his daughter in her maternity nurse scrubs. "That's my Annie."

An hour later, he was the proud father of Sophia Mary and Alexander James Hazard. He couldn't take his eyes off them or his beautiful wife with her mussed hair and streaked makeup. She'd never looked lovelier to him.

"Mommy, Daddy. Are those our babies?" Five-year-old Ian raced into the room. "They're better than Sam. We got two!" He climbed up next to Anne.

Autumn patted him on the shoulder. "Way to go, Dad."

Neal's heart swelled until he thought it would burst. What man could ask for anything more?

* * * * *

*If you enjoyed this story by Jean C. Gordon,
be sure to check out the other books
this month from Love Inspired!*

Dear Reader,

I'm excited about being able to take you back to Paradox Lake in the Adirondack Mountains for Neal Hazard and Anne Howard's story. (You may have met Neal in *Small-Town Sweethearts*.)

We may know God has a plan for us, but we don't always like it or readily accept it. In Neal's case, he thinks he knows and is following God's plan for him. Anne is so uncertain about knowing His plan for her that she's taken things into her own hands. As you may guess, both are in for some surprises.

I hope you enjoy their discoveries about themselves, each other and their faith.

Please feel free to email me at JeanCGordon@yahoo.com or find me on Facebook.

Blessings,
Jean C. Gordon

Questions for Discussion

1. Neal raised his daughter, Autumn, on his own, and now that she's all grown up, he wants to take time out for himself. What do you think of this?

2. Were you surprised that a man like Neal was somewhat intimidated about going back to school? Why? What would your reaction have been?

3. Did you have any experiences—good or bad— as a child that had as great an impact on you as Anne's thunderstorm experience? If so, why do you think it had such a lasting effect?

4. Was Anne right in being cautious about her feelings for Neal, given that he was her student? Why or why not? Was his age a factor or not?

5. When Anne finds out that her friend Reenie made her Ian's guardian, her first reaction is to find a way to not take him home with her. Did this made sense to you? Why or why not? Could you understand her reasons?

6. Do you think Neal's reaction to Anne's initial decision about Ian was too harsh and judgmen-

tal? What changed Anne's heart to make her rethink her decision?

7. Neal realizes that he's more interested in working than in taking college classes. Were you surprised at his decision to not continue his higher education? What do you think you would have done?

8. Anne sees that the Hazards are a close-knit family, and recognizes that she never had that with her parents. Was this a factor in her growing relationship with Neal?

9. Anne is surprised to find that she has friends in Paradox Lake who are willing to help her to raise Ian. Why was Anne so surprised by this?

10. The characters mention the gossip grapevine. Do you think this is something limited to small towns, or do you think it exists everywhere? How does it harm or help a community?

LARGER-PRINT BOOKS!

GET 2 FREE
LARGER-PRINT NOVELS
PLUS 2 FREE
MYSTERY GIFTS

Love Inspired®

Larger-print novels are now available...

LILPDIR13

Love Inspired ®
SUSPENSE
RIVETING INSPIRATIONAL ROMANCE

Watch for our series of edge-
of-your-seat suspense novels.
These contemporary tales
of intrigue and romance
feature Christian characters
facing challenges to their faith...
and their lives!

AVAILABLE IN REGULAR
& LARGER-PRINT FORMATS

For exciting stories that reflect traditional values,
visit:
www.ReaderService.com

ReaderService.com

Manage your account online!

- Review your order history
- Manage your payments
- Update your address

> ### *We've designed the Reader Service website just for you.*

Enjoy all the features!

- Reader excerpts from any series
- Respond to mailings and special monthly offers
- Discover new series available to you
- Browse the Bonus Bucks catalogue
- Share your feedback

Visit us at:

ReaderService.com